"Riveting...Bold...Politically Incorrect! If you like westerns or military thrillers, you'll love *Lone Wolf Canyon*."

—Kevin Sorbo, Actor, Producer, Director, Philanthropist, Author, and Father

"If you are one of those delicate snowflakes who are easily offended...this book is *not* for you. Sherman does a great job of telling a tale that can only be called a modern day western. Unlike anything you have ever read!"

—Jason Mattera, *New York Times* bestselling author

LONE WOLF CANYON

S.C. SHERMAN

Post Hill
PRESS

A POST HILL PRESS BOOK
ISBN: 978-1-68261-549-2
ISBN (eBook): 978-1-68261-550-8

Cover art by Christian Bentulan

Post Hill Press
New York • Nashville
posthillpress.com

Published in the United States of America

Author's Dedication

Some people remember where they were when Kennedy was shot. Depending on your age, others remember what they were doing when the space shuttle Challenger blew up. Most everyone remembers what it felt like when those twin towers fell. I remember the exact moment I heard author Louis L'Amour died.

It was June 10, 1988. I was eighteen years old and I was sleeping in a cheap motel in St. Louis, Missouri. I was part of a travelling construction crew made up of hard cases, drunks, and no account drifters. It was still dark outside when the alarm clock, set to a country music station, went off. No song was playing and the disc jockey announced as if it meant nothing… "Western author Louis L'Amour has died." I bolted upright in the bed. In my head, I screamed…NO!

I was deeply moved, and upset, as if I *knew* him somehow, which I did not. Nobody around me cared, and we had work waiting. I had to stuff my sorrow away and do what any of Louis's characters would've done: saddle up and do what needed done.

My dad was the boss. He ran his crew much like the herd bosses Louis wrote about. It was his way or the highway. He didn't care much what you did at night, but you better be ready to work by sunup. He didn't like slackers. He'd overlook almost anything else, if you worked hard every day. If you didn't hit the bell on time in the morning, he'd draw your wages and fire you on the spot.

I watched Dad fire a man once because he was too drunk or stoned to get out of bed one morning. Dad paid him his due and told him to get out. The man was from Iowa, and we were in West Virginia. The man asked how he was supposed to get home. Dad said, "Not my problem." And we went to work. I last saw that guy bumming a ride from a truck driver.

As we travelled from town-to-town working, I would voraciously read the stories Louis had written. I'd been reading Louis L'Amour westerns since I was in the sixth grade. A friend of mine showed them to me on a shelf in the library. They had about six or eight of them. I selected, *Where the Long Grass Blows*. I was hooked. I read that one and kept on going. Orrin, Tell, and Tyrel Sacket, Milo Talon, Kilkenny, Flint, and all the other characters...they came alive for me. I was just an Iowa farm boy dreaming of being a man someday. I found men in Louis's books I could look up to. The kind of men I wished I could be like, maybe someday.

I can't claim that I've read all of Louis's books, but I've read most of them. Before I fell in love with Louis' westerns, I read Walter Farley's Black Stallion book series, and after Louis I moved on to Tom Clancy's war games type books. Of all those authors who shaped my youth, Louis L'Amour did the most.

I can say that those boyhood dreams of riding the rails, busting a bronc, or watching my back against a Clinch Mountain Sackett still haunt me today. I long for an adventure on the far-off hills, and I probably always will.

The story contained here is a story set in the West, as all good stories are. A tale of a lost place with a history crashing headlong into the present-day dramas that unfold all around us.

Since I became an author, I've never dared to write a western, until now. This story is meant to be a modern day western. It is not a book Louis would have written. I left *in* the vulgar language of rough men, as it is how they talk. It is my sincere hope that Louis would have enjoyed this tale, and I hope that you enjoy it as well.

Thank you for all the stories, my hero, Louis L'Amour.

There will come a time when you

believe everything is finished.

Yet that will be the beginning.

–Louis L'Amour

Special Thanks

I would like to personally thank Rick Dennis, Drew Sherman, Jack Sherman, and Jack and Deb Frost for their support and encouragement with *Lone Wolf Canyon*. Some special thanks for their military expertise to Gabe Haugland, Combat Veteran, Afghanistan and Major Kyle Obrecht, Executive Officer, 224th Engineer Battalion.

TABLE OF CONTENTS

CHAPTER 1

DISCHARGE

"Do you want a cigarette?"

"I don't smoke."

"Really, well you're in the minority amongst your peers," the middle-aged woman said, quickly glancing at her notes. This patient's piercing brown eyes were unnerving. Even though he was easily ten years her younger, his good looks were obvious. She tried to mask her attraction to him. She glanced at her papers and then quickly up at him again. He was dark and rugged looking. She could sense he was a dangerous man. She focused on her work.

"Well, let's get started. I am Dr. Lattry. It's my job to see how you're doing. Help you adjust back to the regular world."

"What if I don't need help?" the young man stated without adjusting his gaze. His appearance was perfect. Precise military style. Everything in order. His dark hair cropped close, posture—ramrod straight and strong. Speech—direct and to the point.

"Everyone needs help sometime. Please state your name and rank. I have a series of questions I'm required to ask you," Dr. Lattry continued with a shake of her head. His arrogance reminded her that he was just another mother's son acting the man.

She was getting tired of the constant games in these interviews. *Only one more month and I'm out of here too,* she thought and on to a sweet job in private practice. She could finally let her hair down and make some serious money.

"State your name and rank," she reminded.

"Sergeant Lance Hamilton, Sniper, Sniper Team Leader, 3rd Ranger Battalion, 75th Regiment, Fort Benning," he stated proudly.

"So, you're a sniper?" Dr. Lattry asked as she checked a box on the document spread out before her on the table.

"Yes, ma'am."

"Lance, may I call you Lance?"

"Sure, but no one else does."

"What do they call you?"

"Ham."

"May I call you Ham?"

"Yes, ma'am.

"Ham, are you looking forward to being a regular citizen again?"

"I guess, but I'll always be a Ranger."

"Yes, I know, it's a brotherhood. You're not the first Ranger I've met," the doctor said with a slight eye roll that bothered Ham. He felt the corner of his mouth twitch with anger. He focused his attention to conceal all external signs that she was bothering him. He knew he had to get through this interview without an outburst or they'd be all over him. His anger was closer to the surface than it used to be.

"What are your plans Lance, I mean Ham? It says here you have no family, your mom died of cancer when you were a teenager, but you were raised by an aunt from Texas?"

"Yes, Aunt Shirley, she's gone too. Uvalde, Texas. That's where I grew up, mostly. I have friends there. I worked as a hunting guide on a ranch. They'll take me back."

"You have a job lined up then?"

"Well, I haven't talked to them yet, but when I left they said come back after I get out and I'll always have a job."

"What if they won't take you back? How would that make you feel?" The doctor stared right into his eyes waiting for his reaction as much as his response.

He smiled and met her gaze. Finally, she had some sand after all.

"I guess that would make me feel unemployed," Lance answered slowly, enjoying the game. He was confident she couldn't read him. He had no intention of going back to Texas. He had no job waiting and no friends who would miss him. He'd seen on Facebook, the only girl who ever showed any interest in him was married to the hardware store owner and had three kids. He did have a plan, but he wasn't going to share it with this headshrinker.

"What happened to your father? He's not mentioned in here."

The smile left Ham's face. "He left when I was little."

"Left?" she could sense his unease.

"Yes, left."

"You've had no contact with him?"

"He's dead. Fell off a bridge in New Orleans. Drunk. Good riddance."

"How old were you when he left?"

"What does this have to do with my discharge?"

"Just evaluating your state of mind. Abandonment as a child can exacerbate symptoms of PTSD in returning soldiers. It's relevant, now answer the question."

"I was eight. He beat the crap out of my mom so bad, he shattered her eye socket. So, when he fell asleep, I hit him in the head with a hammer. If I'd have been older, and a little stronger, I'd have killed him. Instead, he just had a concussion, and when they let him out of the hospital, he packed up his stuff and left, but not before he gave me a goodbye present."

"What was that?"

Ham raised his hand and pointed to the two-inch scar over his left eye just below the eye brow. "Seriously, that was a long time ago. Don't cry for me, alright. He's dead. My mom's dead. I've been in a long time, and I just want to go home and hunt deer," he softened his face as he tried to manipulate her.

"Fine, how are you handling your symptoms?"

"What symptoms?

"Anxiety, depression, suicidal thoughts, triggers from loud noises, smells, bad dreams, you name it. How are you handling it?"

"I'm fine. I've been handling that stuff all my life. You won't find me balled up in a corner. I'm right as rain," he said with a glance around the room as if he wanted to bolt. He hated rooms with no windows. He could feel his anxiety level going through the roof. It was all he could do to keep from looking at her like he wanted to kill her. He quickly imagined taking the pen from her hand and stabbing her in the neck with it. He consciously held his hand still as he could feel it starting to nervously twitch.

"I'm going to find you a counselor in Texas who specializes in PTSD therapy. I will set up your first appointment. You need to talk about your emotions if you want to get back to a normal life," Dr. Lattry was writing as she spoke.

"Normal life, yes ma'am."

"Don't joke around. Do you know how high the suicide rate for returning vets is? Men just as tough as you. Men just as arrogant as you, who thought they were fine. You're not fine. There's a lot you're not telling me. Get counseling or suffer. It's up to you."

"Thank you for your analysis, Doc."

She just shook her head, signed a statement, and handed him a sheet of paper. "Thank you for your service. Get counseling. I'm not kidding."

"Thank you for your concern. I'm free to go?"

"Yes, you can go," she said returning to her paperwork.

Ham stood, turned on his heel, and left as quickly as he could. Almost free.

Ham went to his locker and pulled out a well-worn sheet of paper. Mac had printed it off at the base in Afghanistan. He read it out loud to himself under his breath. He'd long since memorized it, but he read it anyway.

Full Time Wrangler Wanted. Room, board, and horse included. Long days, low pay, isolation, no phone service, no Wi-Fi, bad food, poor conditions followed by on and off horse work that never ends. If interested apply in person at Lost Circus Ranch, River of No Return, Idaho. If you can't find it, you're not the guy.

It was their plan. Mac had found the job posting on some obscure web site. He said, "If we make it back alive, we're gonna find Lost Circus Ranch." They were going to find it together, but he was alone now. He'd felt alone most of his life. Mac was the only true friend he'd ever had. The Lost Circus Ranch was going to be their adventure together after they'd left the hell of the 'Stan behind. Mac grew up on a Nebraska cattle ranch; they shared a love of horses, hunting, cows, and the great outdoors.

His eyes glazed over into a stare. He could see it. Blood everywhere. He could smell the burning nitrate. His eyes stung. His left arm hung limp at his side. Mac's head lay in his lap; his legs were gone. Gunfire exploded all around them. Mac had frothy blood on his lips and he stared straight into Ham's eyes. "Promise me you'll find it. Promise me…Lost Circus…"

"I promise…" Ham whispered. He shook his head and blinked his eyes back to the present.

He'd searched the internet for the post, but it was nowhere to be found. The print out Mac had printed was more than a year old, but he was going anyway. A promise sealed in blood, is a promise to be kept.

Ham had researched the area. The Frank Church—River of No Return Wilderness was one of the largest National Parks in the United States. Encompassing 2.4 million acres of untamed wilderness. Only a few privately owned ranches remained landlocked by unmolested government-owned ground. Most of them only attainable by the river or by air.

He read a description of the area from wilderness.net. He'd read it a hundred times before. It read like a dream. A dream of a lost place calling to his heart. *Come and find me.*

The Frank Church—River of No Return is a land of clear rivers, deep canyons, and rugged mountains. Two white-water rivers draw many human visitors: The Main Salmon River, which runs west near the northern boundary; and the Middle Fork of the Salmon, which begins near the southern boundary and runs north for about 104 miles until it joins the Main. Reaching 6,300 feet from the river bottom, the canyon carved by the Main Salmon is deeper than most of the earth's canyons—including the Grand Canyon of the Colorado River—and this fast-moving waterway has been dubbed the River of No Return. In the northeastern corner of the Wilderness, the Selway River flows north into the nearby Selway-Bitterroot Wilderness. Trout fishing usually rates from good to excellent. The Middle Fork, the Selway, and nearly all of the Main Salmon are Wild and Scenic Rivers. Unlike the sheer walls of the Grand Canyon, these rivers rush below wooded ridges rising steeply toward the sky, beneath eroded bluffs and ragged, solitary crags. The Salmon River Mountains dominate the interior of the Wilderness. Without a major crest, these mountains splay out in a multitude of minor crests in all directions, and rise gradually to wide summits. East of the Middle Fork, the fabulous Bighorn Crags form a jagged series of summits, at least one topping 10,000 feet. The Crags surround 14 strikingly beautiful clearwater lakes. Hiking up from the rivers into the mountains brings sudden elevation changes. Great forests of Douglas Fir and Lodge Pole Pine cover much of the area, with spruce and fir higher up and ponderosa pine at lower altitudes. The forests are broken by grassy meadows and sun-washed, treeless slopes. A dry country, as little as 10 inches of precipitation falls near the rivers. As much as 50 inches may fall on the mountaintops, but much of it is snow. Despite the dryness, wildlife abounds. As many as 370 species have been identified in a single year, including eight big game animals.

He sifted through his copies of the topo and satellite maps he'd printed. He squinted at the images that were so clear you could see pine trees and cattle. The main house sat well back from the river. Even in the satellite images the place looked rundown and unkempt. Old fencing could be seen, as well as at least two buildings that had all but collapsed. He wondered what sort of man ran an ad like that. He was hell bent to find out.

He stuffed his papers into his duffel and zipped it shut. Everything else he owned, which consisted of a variety of uniforms, some awards, an old TV, and trunk of personals was safely locked in storage. It felt strange being in plain clothes on the base. He shouldered his duffel and turned his back to all he'd known for what seemed like forever.

"Well, here we go," he whispered to himself as he climbed into a yellow cab.

"To the airport," he said as Fort Benning disappeared in the rear-view mirror. The future sprawled out before him like a blank canvas, while the past pressed firmly upon his chest as a weight threatening suffocation and always invisibly there.

Ham sat silently in the airport. He stared at his phone. Flicking the screen with his finger and reading posts. He didn't look up. He didn't want to talk to anyone. Suddenly, a flight attendant stood before him.

"Excuse me," she asked.

"Yes," he answered.

"You are invited to board first as thanks for your service," she said with a smile.

"Thank you. It's not necessary," he said as he put his phone away and shouldered his pack. She led off toward the gate. He handed them his ticket. They processed it and gave the stubs back to him. The flight attendant motioned for him to go on ahead. He felt a little guilty boarding first. He hadn't done anything that wasn't expected of him. He didn't feel like anyone special. He found his window seat, stowed his gear, and sat down watching the ground crew load the bags.

The plane slowly filled with passengers. The other two seats in his row were filled with a mother and her boy. The boy looked to be about ten and sat next to him with his mother on the aisle. The boy stared at him with big blue eyes.

The boy noticed Ham's cap with the single word, RANGER, emblazoned in gold. "What's a Ranger?" the boy asked.

"A kind of soldier," Ham replied with a smile and wink.

"Are you like Captain America?" the boy continued as they rose to cruising altitude.

"No, I wish I had a shield like that though."

"What's that?" the little boy pointed to the black lines tattooed into Ham's forearm.

Ham pushed his shirt up to display the entire tattoo. "This one is Arabic for *Infidel.* You'll have to ask your mom what that means."

The boy looked to his mom. "Later," she said with a smile and went back to her magazine.

"Here, look at this one," Ham said as he rolled up his other sleeve revealing a bashful pink pig cartoon image.

"Porky Pig," the boy exclaimed.

"He's so old, I wasn't sure you'd know him," Ham said with a smile.

"You like Porky Pig?" the boy asked.

"My name is Ham. Ham comes from pigs. See how that is kinda funny?"

The kid wrinkled his nose and shook his head *no* as if he didn't get it. "Did you kill people?"

His mother gasped. "Oh my, I'm sorry," she exclaimed.

"Really, it's okay," Ham said.

"We don't ask questions like that," she scolded her son.

Ham winked at the little boy. "Only bad guys."

Ham's hand twitched. In his mind flashed a dead boy no older than this boy next to him. The dead boy's young face was surprisingly serene. The top of his head had been removed by Ham's shot. His little body wrapped in undetonated explosives. He felt the pat on his back as someone said in a muffled voice, "Good shot, Ham." The acrid smell of gun powder filled his nostrils.

He was startled back to reality with a jump.

The flight attendant stood in the aisle with the cart. "Do you want anything, sir?"

"Two gin and tonics."

"Okay, here you go," she handed him two little plastic airline bottles of gin. "All we have is Sprite. Is that okay?"

"Yes, fine. Thanks."

She popped the top of the Sprite and handed him the can and a cup of ice. The boy and the mother had a Sprite as well, but no gin.

Ham dumped both gin bottles into the cup and splashed the remaining space with Sprite. He immediately tipped it up and drank the bulk of the clear liquid. "Aahh."

He suddenly noticed both the boy and his mother were staring at him.

"I'm really thirsty," he said sheepishly. He poured some more Sprite into the cup, took a sip, and turned to stare out the window. He could faintly see beautiful green squares passing by like a giant patchwork quilt that is the Midwest.

"Flyover country," he whispered. He emptied his cup as he realized he was flying over Nebraska. Mac's parents were down there somewhere.

I'll go see them...after...after I find the Lost Circus, he thought. He wished he could have another gin, but the flight attendant was nowhere to be seen. Not to mention he didn't want to scare the little boy next to him any more than he already had. He put his head back and closed his eyes feigning sleep. It wasn't long until they started their descent.

CHAPTER 2

"Bye, bye," the little boy said with a wave. His mother ushered him off the plane as fast as she could.

"Enjoy your stay in Boise," the flight attendant said to Ham as he quietly filed by on his way off the plane. Ham just smiled and nodded.

Ham had no checked baggage so he exited the airport without delay. The Idaho air was crisp and clear. Temperature was ideal. Something about the wind just *tasted* good. In the distance, mountains rose into the hazy sky.

"The Wild West," Ham said with a smile. He raised his hand and a taxi quickly stopped in front of him. He climbed in.

An overweight man with long silver hair cleared his meter and glanced in the rear-view mirror. His shoulders were covered in an abundance of white flakes. His black Def Leppard t-shirt did nothing but accentuate his dandruff. Ham didn't care.

"Where to, sir?"

"No 'sir' necessary," Ham said.

"I was a private once, about 200 pounds ago," the driver said with a laugh. "I know a superior officer when I see one."

"Just got out. I'm a citizen, just like you. I need a hotel and a meal," Ham said. "I have no reservations."

"I know just the place, gives a military discount and a great steakhouse right across the street," the driver said as he pulled away.

"Sounds perfect," Ham answered. "Anyplace I can rent a car to get to Salmon?"

"I know a guy who drives a truck, does a run up there once a week on his way to Helena. He goes tomorrow. I'm sure he'd let you hitch along for nothing."

"Sounds good to me. Can he pick me up at the hotel?"

"Let me call him," the driver said as he put a phone to his head.

"What's up, Tyler?" the driver said into the phone. "I got a serviceman that needs a ride to Salmon. You heading there tomorrow?...Can you pick him up at the Wagon Wheel?...Thanks. What time?...Catch you later."

After hanging up, the driver tossed his phone into his lap and glanced into the rear-view mirror. "He said he could pick you up there, but it will be early...like 5 a.m."

"0500. I'll be in the lobby. Thanks," Ham said.

"Thank you for your service," the driver said as he pulled into a hotel with a huge wagon wheel covering the front entrance. "Here you go. Ten bucks."

Ham handed him a twenty. "Keep the change. Thanks for your help."

"No problem. Go get a steak right over there," he said as he pointed to a rustic looking building with a rearing stallion lit up in neon. *Red Stallion Steakhouse.*

"I will. Thanks again," Ham said as he climbed out and shouldered his pack. He shut the door and made his way into the hotel lobby.

A young man dressed in denim sat up as he entered. "Welcome to the Wagon Wheel."

"Thanks, got a room?" Ham asked.

"We do. Just you?"

"Yep, just me."

The young man slid a metal key attached to a diamond shaped plastic key chain with the number seven on it.

"Number seven is right down the hall on this floor. Pool is closed for repairs, but it's been closed all year. Don't expect it to open soon."

"No big deal. I just need a place to sleep," Ham said with a smile. "Got a clean bed?"

"Yes, well, pretty clean. Also, I see your cap, are you a Ranger?"

"Yes, I just got out."

"Ten percent off military discount," the young man said. "It's $54."

Ham paid in cash and took the key. He turned his back on the young man as he looked like he wanted to say more and Ham was done talking for today.

The room was clean. That was the best part. The rest of it was old. It looked like it hadn't been updated since it was new in the 80s. Ham bolted and chained the door. He didn't like the big windows facing the street. The curtain was sheer and let a lot of light in. He found that jiggling one of the windows caused it to unlock and fall open. Ham grabbed a roll of duct tape from his pack. He shut the window and duct taped the latch shut to keep it from falling open.

"Nobody around here wants to kill you," he said to himself. "This is Boise fricking Idaho. If you can't be safe here, we're doomed." He suddenly realized he was hungry and a steak didn't sound half bad. It might be his last good meal if the ad lived up to its promise of *bad food.*

Ham took a quick shower and put on a pair of Wranglers and a buttoned-down shirt. He was a civilian now. Might as well look like one. His uniformed days were behind him. He slapped his cap back on his head. "I need to get a proper cowboy hat before I head out," he said to his reflection in the mirror.

He dropped his key in his pocket. He suddenly wished he was armed. Old habits die hard. Instead, he listened through the door. No one in the hall. He stepped out and shut the door behind him. He checked that the door was locked, then carefully stuck a toothpick between the door and the frame near the corner on the hinge side. If anyone opened the door while he was gone, he'd know it.

He made his way quickly down the hall and exited through the lobby before the young man had a chance to speak again. He was staring down at his phone and didn't even notice Ham until he was almost out the front door.

A pickup truck threw gravel as it fishtailed across the parking lot with country music blasting out the window. The lot was surprisingly full as Ham made his way between the cars. He felt the tension rise in the back of his neck. He wished he was armed with more than his knife, but it would have to do. A couple of people sat on a tailgate sharing a smoke. Others were coming and going. Ham caught himself assessing everything as a threat as if he was going out on patrol again.

"No one cares about you going to dinner," he whispered to himself. "Old habits die hard. It's gonna take some time." No one noticed him as he stepped into the restaurant and moved to the sidewall, eyes scanning the room for threats. The place was all country. A cowboy band was playing in front of a wooden dance floor that already had a few folks two-stepping. The lead singer had a flannel shirt with the top four buttons undone and was just laying into *Whiskey Bent and Hell Bound*. His voice was marginal, but no one seemed to care. The beer was flowing and people were laughing.

Ham noticed that the restaurant was divided into two sides. One side had booths and tables looking like a restaurant, while the other side was a long bar complete with a full-length mirror and ornate carvings making it all honky-tonk. A middle-aged waitress wearing "Daisy Dukes" whisked by and gave Ham a wink, "Hon, you eatin' or drinkin'?"

"Eatin'," he answered. "And drinkin'."

She pointed to a small booth in the corner, "You can have that one if you like?"

He nodded *yes* and quickly proceeded to his table. It was perfectly located with a solid wall behind him and a good view of the dance floor and both exits he'd noticed. He sat down and put his cap in his lap.

Daisy Duke was suddenly back, "What can I get you sweetie?"

"I want a steak, ribeye, medium rare, baked potato, butter and sour cream, raw horseradish if you have it, none of that mixed stuff, and a salad with ranch out first, and bring me two Bud heavies right away," Ham said as he stared straight into her eyes.

"Wow, a man who knows what he wants. Where you been all my life?" she chuckled. "I wish there were more like you. I'll have the beers right out, and it's your lucky day. Happy hour is on for another twenty minutes, and beers are 2 for 1. Here's some peanuts to snack on," she said as she handed him a Folgers Coffee can full of salted peanuts. Ham had already noticed the crunch of peanut shells on the floor.

He watched her walk away. "They don't have places like this in Bagram," he said to himself. He continued scanning every person in the room. Only a couple toughs worth any worry. He noticed three people poorly carrying concealed, and one woman who looked to be the most dangerous person in the room. He could see it in her eyes, cold. It didn't take long until the steak arrived.

"Here you go, hon. I brought you a couple more beers before happy hour quits," Daisy said with a smile. The aroma of the steak triggered a sharp pain in Ham's stomach. It looked good.

"Thanks." He finished off the second of the first two beers and handed her the empty cans.

"Grab me if you need anything," she said as she trotted off about her work. She seemed perfectly suited for her job.

"Been a long time since I had a steak like this," he whispered. "God bless America." Ham devoured his steak, hardly taking a breath. It was succulent. "The cab driver was right. A great steak," he said to himself.

Daisy returned and noticed he was already done. "You wolfed that right down! Hungry huh?"

"Sure was. It was good too!"

She sat a shot glass of amber colored liquor in front of him.

"This is from the ladies at the bar over there." Daisy pointed to two women sitting at the bar holding their shot glasses in the air and smiling at him ear-to-ear.

He shook his head. "Oh boy, I shouldn't," he whispered. "But I'm gonna." He took the shot glass between his thumb and forefinger and raised it to them. He gave them a smile and slammed it back. The tequila burned as it delivered its power home. As the warmth spread across his chest the two girls slid into the booth one on either side of him.

"You're new around here," The one with the blonde curls said. Her speech was already slightly impaired, but it did not diminish her attractiveness. "I'm Kenzie, and this is Julie."

She pointed to her brunette friend. Julie batted her brown eyes and sheepishly looked away. "Julie acts shy, but she thinks you're hot. She's the one who wanted to send you the shot." Ham turned his head and smiled at Julie.

"Thank you, Julie. I haven't had a beautiful girl buy me a shot in a long time," Ham smiled at her with a hungry look. Julie felt the blood rush to her head and her cheeks flushed.

"So what's your name?" Kenzie asked.

"My friends call me Ham," he said.

"Ham? Like the meat?" Kenzie squealed.

"Yes, my name is Lance Hamilton. Get it? Ham, short for Hamilton?"

"Okay, maybe I'll call you Bacon. I love bacon," Kenzie laughed.

"Don't do that," he said with a serious glance that let Kenzie know he wasn't kidding.

"What are you doing here Ham-bone? What brings you to Idaho?" Kenzie continued.

"I am on some personal business," Ham answered.

"You don't look like a businessman," she questioned. "What are you up to? Gold mining?"

"No. I just got out of the military, and I'm on a personal business matter for a friend," Ham said.

"Where's your friend? Is he cute?" Kenzie said with a glance around the room.

Ham chuckled and shook his head. "You'd have thought he was cute. I dearly wish he was here. He would of liked you, but he's dead," Ham said. He paused as the emotion was closer to the surface than Ham had expected. Ham focused hard on his beer as he pushed it down. Kenzie glanced at Julie across the table, uneasy tension filling the air.

"Let's have another shot!" Ham said with a robust fist pound to the table.

"Woohoo!" Kenzie hollered. "Sounds good!"

A couple more shots, and Julie slipped her hand onto Ham's thigh under the table. Kenzie excused herself to the dance floor.

"I'm sorry about Kenzie being so forward," Julie said. "We come here almost every Friday after work, and she always has men hitting on her. She's always trying to set me up. I'm sorry."

"I'm not. I wouldn't have met you if she hadn't been so…"

"Forward," Julie said with a giggle.

"Yeah, forward," Ham answered. His own words were slurring a bit and his face was flush. He wasn't watching the door so much. His eyes were on Julie now. He suddenly leaned forward and her lips were on his.

They kissed deeply as if no one else was in the room. He opened his eyes and leaned back. "I'm sorry. I don't usually drink this much."

"I'm not sorry. So you wouldn't kiss me if you weren't drunk?" she asked.

"No, I would kiss you, drunk or sober."

"Yeah, right," she said looking a little hurt.

"I would kiss you sober. Seriously, you're beautiful. I can't believe you'd kiss me," he said.

"Stop it. Any girl in here would kiss you."

"I wouldn't kiss any of them." Daisy walked by and Ham motioned to her. "Well maybe her."

Julie slapped his shoulder and he laughed.

"Where you from soldier?" she said changing the subject.

"Texas originally, most recently Fort Benning, Georgia, but we aren't talking about me tonight. Where are you from?"

"Idaho, all my life. Pocatello originally, but I've been working here in Boise since high school. I went to a year of community college. It wasn't for me."

Daisy suddenly appeared with four more shots and a couple more Buds. "From Kenzie," she said.

They could see Kenzie on the dance floor grinding with some cowboy. She was smiling and waving at them.

"She's a good friend. Just a little crazy," Julie said.

Ham lifted a shot. "To Kenzie. To crazy good friends. There aren't that many of them."

Julie clinked her glass against Ham's, and they both downed the liquid. Julie coughed after swallowing as she choked to hold the strong liquor down. She laughed and nestled in closer to Ham. "I don't normally drink this much."

Ham suddenly checked his watch. "2330 hours. Man, I gotta go. I gotta get some sleep. My ride is gonna be here at 0500."

"Your ride? Where are you going?" Julie asked.

"River of No Return." The booze kept him talking. "Lost Circus Ranch."

"Lost Circus Ranch? Never heard of that one. I thought I'd heard of all of them up there," Julie said. "It's beautiful out here, you're going to love it if you like the outdoors."

"I'm gonna be working out there for a while. Maybe a long while. No phone, no internet, no contact," he said. His eyes were blinking slowly.

"Well, when you finally come back from the river, will you call me?" She slid a business card toward him. On one side it had her phone number in blue ink with a heart at the end. The other side stated: The Hair Depot, Julie McClure, Stylist Extraordinaire.

"Stylist Extraordinaire?" he raised an eyebrow.

"Yeah, Kenzie said it sounds better that way. Like we do more than cut and color hair."

"My aunt raised me for a while. She cut hair. I like it," Ham said. He took the card and slid it into his shirt pocket. "When I come back from the river, I will call you."

They kissed again. Finally, Ham stood to go.

Julie stuck out her lip as if she was pouting that he was leaving.

"I don't want to go. I have to get some sleep. Remember, my ride comes early?" Ham said.

She stood and gave him one last kiss. After they were done she patted his chest. "I won't expect you to call, but I'd like it if you did."

"I'll call. You can count on that. Chances are, you won't remember me." They stared into each other's eyes for a moment. Ham didn't know what to do. Should he kiss her again or what? Suddenly, he just nodded and turned on his heel and marched right out the front door. When the cool night air hit his face, he realized he was drunk. The world was spinning a bit and his steps were not in cadence.

"Good thing I don't have far to go," he whispered to himself.

He shuffled in the front door of the Wagon Wheel and didn't even notice the desk clerk as he made his way to his room.

He glanced at the toothpick right where he'd left it. Nobody had opened the door. As he pulled out his key, he dropped it. He bent to pick it up and suddenly a slender hand snatched it up. He jumped back and raised his hands to block the blow he anticipated coming hard.

"It's your lucky night, soldier. Lucky number seven," Julie said with a smile. She inserted the key into the knob and opened the door, stepping inside. Ham followed her in, shutting the door behind him. He worked the dead bolt and added the chain. He turned and saw Julie. She stood naked in the moonlight as it shimmered through the sheer curtains. "Whoa," he stammered at the sight of her.

"Whoa?" she repeated.

"I mean, wow, you're beautiful," he said.

"I don't do this...I've really never done this. Well, I mean I've done *it*, just not this, because we hardly know each other, but something's different about you," she continued to talk nervously and suddenly crossed her arms to partially cover herself. "I shouldn't have come."

Ham took her hands and looked into her eyes. "I don't take this lightly. I'm glad you came. Now when I'm out on the river all I will think of is you." He took her in his arms, and they kissed passionately.

"You're drunk," she said.

"Maybe a little. I told you I need to get some sleep," Ham whispered.

She pushed him onto the bed. "After."

His head was pounding as he sat on the edge of the bath tub and wrote a note on Wagon Wheel stationary. It read.

Julie,

When I get back from the river I'll be calling. Count on it!

Ham.

He opened the bathroom door letting the light pour into the room. Ham paused and looked at Julie as she slept. He gently brushed the hair from her cheek and left the note on the table by the bed. He shut off the light, shouldered his pack, and quietly eased out of the hotel room, shutting the door as silently as he could.

There was black coffee in a pot in the lobby. Ham poured himself a Styrofoam cup. It was horrible, but it was steaming hot. Ham slammed a solid drink of the black sludge, burning his tongue in the process. He nodded at the older woman sitting quietly behind the counter knitting to pass the long night. His eyes burned and were red and swollen from the tequila. He smiled just a bit as he caught a subtle whiff of Julie's perfume on his clothes. The cold night air felt good as he sat down on the bench out front. He glanced at his watch. 0505.

"He's late," Ham said. Just then bright headlights from a straight truck pulled into the parking lot. Large letters on the side read: *Boise All Natural Produce.*

The big diesel stopped abruptly, and the driver rolled down his window. He was a young man. Barely old enough to sprout a whisker and so slender Ham wondered if he could handle such a big truck.

"You the guy looking for a ride to Salmon?" His voice was shockingly low for such a youthful appearance.

"That's me," Ham said.

"Hop in," the driver hollered and began rolling up his window. "We're off. Got a schedule to keep."

Ham looked back at the hotel one last time. He could just stay right here. Go back inside, marry Julie, and make a home. Why did he have to leave? She was warm and nestled in to a comfortable bed. Right there waiting for him. Why not forget chasing old ghosts and promises to the dead?

He shook his head, locked his jaw, and sealed his determination. He'd promised Mac. He had it to do. Ham climbed up into the big truck, in search of the unknown.

CHAPTER 3

SALMON

"The name's Slim," the driver said as he stuck out his hand. Ham met his gaze and gave his hand a shake. He may have been skinny, but his hand was like iron. He had a strong grip and an honest way about him that Ham liked right away.

"You can call me Ham."

"Ham. Got it. So where'd you serve?"

"Here and there. Mostly in the 'Stan."

"Iraq or Afghanistan?

"Both."

"Did we do any good over there?"

"Yeah, for some of the people. They're dirt ass poor in the villages. They suffer from whoever's in power. Killing Saddam and Osama were good things, but more just like them come along and fill in the voids. It's tribal. Been going on for centuries. Strength is all that matters. Brutal mostly."

"So what's it really like for you guys?"

"Fucking hot, and rocky and sandy," Ham said with a smile.

Slim laughed out loud, "Don't doubt that! Fuck that place! You're back in the US of A now. What you doing up in Salmon?"

"Gotta find a place called the Lost Circus Ranch about a job."

"It's on the main fork of the Salmon?"

"Yeah, I guess."

"Never heard of it. I can send you to a guy who would know. He knows everybody out in The Church. Used to be an outfitter before everybody started doing it with these jet boats. He used to fly people in and drop 'em off, then pick 'em up downstream. If anybody knows the place you're looking for… it'd be him. Ole Lloyd, he's quite a character too. You'll like him. He was military back in the day."

"Thanks. How long 'til we get to Salmon?"

"About five hours, give or take a bit."

"Mind if I rest? I went for a steak at the Red Stallion and got a little more than I bargained for. My heads fuckin' killing me."

"What was her name?"

"Julie and Jose Cuervo," Ham said as he stared out the window noticing the eastern peaks outlined in subtle light.

"Don't know Julie, but I've had a run in or two with that bastard Jose!"

"He's not a friend of mine," Ham laughed.

"Get some shut eye. I'm used to driving alone. This truck's not the best place for a nap. She's rough as a cob."

"I've napped in worse. I can promise you that."

Slim turned on the radio, and Ham laid his head back on the seat rest, slightly pulling his cap down to his eyebrows. The truck bounced and jostled along, but it didn't take long for Ham to fall asleep. The big diesel had a rhythm he liked, not to mention almost no risk of driving over a road side bomb. That truth was enough to induce a very peaceful rest.

Ham opened his eyes several hours later and silently watched the breathtaking scenery roll by as if it was nothing. He caught a glimpse of some elk grazing on a hillside of green grass and rock outcroppings. Mountains covered in pine accented by lush meadows with winding streams made for a picturesque view. Old homesteads and broken down irrigation systems long abandoned hinted at the harshness of this country cloaked in beauty. Ham was happy that Slim didn't have to talk. Another hour passed without them speaking to each other. Slim lit one cigarette from the next and hummed along with each country music song on the radio. Ham was content with his thoughts and the countryside rolling by.

His thoughts lingered on Julie. He could see her in his mind and wished he was heading back to Boise. He remembered everything about his time with her, as if he'd been sober as a church mouse. She wasn't the first girl he'd known, but there was something different about her. A softness, born of a harsh world.

Slim lit a new cigarette and tossed the butt of his old one out the window. "I don't normally smoke this much, but the lighter in the truck is broken so I can't let it go out," he said with a laugh. Both men knew it was a lie.

"You could buy a lighter at a gas station," Ham answered.

"Good idea. Thanks." He pointed out the side window. "Just over the next rise we'll come into Salmon. My stop is a little all natural grocery. A nice mom and pop shop. Right next door to a great café, if you're hungry."

"Starving."

"I can point you to Ol' Lloyd too. He'll be able to find the place you're looking for."

"That'd be great. You gonna eat at the café?" Ham asked. "I'm buying."

"No, I gotta keep rolling. I'm going on to Helena."

Ham noticed a sign:

Welcome to Salmon
Population 3112

The quaint mountain town was suddenly around them. Trucks pulling trailers loaded with blue rafts were everywhere. He noticed fly fishing shops, hiking outfitters, a pawn shop, a couple pizza places, a few bars, a real estate company, and many more rafts.

"Salmon's a nice little town. The Church provides all kinds of tourists. The Salmon River is like life to this little piece of the world. Without the river, nothing would be going on out here. It's a good place to live," Slim said as he pulled into a parking lot and backed up to a loading dock.

"The café is right over there." He pointed.

Ham stuck his hand out and they shook hands firmly, eyes locked. "Thanks for the ride. What do I owe ya?"

Slim laughed, "You can pay me when you see me again."

A big grin grew across Ham's face. "I reckon so."

With another boisterous laugh, Slim hopped out of his truck and was off to see about his load.

Ham opened the passenger door and climbed out. He shouldered his pack, with a glance behind. Slim was already heading into the back door of the grocery.

An antique-looking sign hung over the café that had the look of an old west boardwalk styled building. Ham liked it right off. Stenciled in a font like cave dwellers would use were the words: *Sacajawea Café and Coffee...Find your way.*

Ham stepped in and quickly surveyed the threats in the room. Two older men in cowboy garb leaned in close and were talking. The one who could see him took note. His aged appearance belied a tough old bird. Ham noticed a faded Globe and Anchor tattooed on his forearm.

A long counter presented itself before him. Only a couple people sat with their backs to Ham and the door. Neither of them even bothered to look. A middle-aged couple and their three children occupied a table and were making a lot of noise as two of the children were screaming at each other. The mother looked frazzled. "I don't care if the ketchup from your fries touched your bun, you're eating it!" she yelled at her child. She had tried to keep her voice down, but the anger increased her volume. Her tirade ended with her hand slamming on the table. The husband caught the water glass before it rolled to the floor. Her child crossed her arms and slumped back into her chair, a frown on her face.

"C'mon in," a waitress said as she handed Ham a menu. "Don't mind them. They're enjoying their vacay...can't you tell?" She laughed. "You can sit at the counter if you like."

"That's fine," Ham noticed a seat at one end with a good view of the room. He took the menu and sat down.

The waitress went behind the counter. "What can I get you?"

"Coffee. Black and hot."

"What else is there?" she asked with a smile and a wink. "Stand a fork in it."

"You serving breakfast or lunch?"

"We serve breakfast all day every day, so get what you like."

"I'll take the western omelet with hash browns and bacon." Ham handed her his menu.

"Anything else?"

"You got sausage?"

"Of course."

"Links or patties?"

"Links."

"I'll take some links too."

"Coming right up."

Bacon and sausage always seemed to wipe away a hangover.

Ham noticed a newspaper laying on the counter. He picked it up and read the headlines.

The Recorder Herald
Two Rescued in Fire and New Restaurant Opens

Ham chuckled to himself as he started reading the local news. He noticed there was not one story about the Middle East and that was fine with him. That was all behind him now. Maybe this is the kind of place he could get lost in? Maybe it was perfect? He wished Mac was sitting right here next to him, but he wasn't.

The door jingled as it opened. Ham glanced over his paper, but didn't move it. He took a deep breath and felt his pulse quicken. The first man through the door was a big man, easily 250 pounds of muscle, and he handled himself smoothly on his feet. He had a broad face and a strong chin. His hair was cropped close, and his brown skin was the color of mahogany.

He quickly surveyed the room, and his dark eyes settled on Ham. Ham knew he would be trouble. Two more men followed, they were both Middle Eastern in appearance. Ham had seen it a thousand times before. He thought he was having a flashback it was so real. They wore traditional Middle Eastern clothes and walked with the air of confidence he'd grown to detest. The man in the middle was obviously in charge. It wasn't just the gray in his beard that gave it away. Everything about him exuded leadership.

The waitress sat Ham's food down in front of him oblivious about what was going on. "A western omelet, bacon, hash browns, and a side of links. Anything else I can get you?"

Ham didn't look at his food. It smelled wonderful. His stomach growled. "I'll take a coffee refill."

The black man walked right toward Ham. He maintained eye contact as he approached. Ham carefully folded up his paper and set it aside. He glanced at his food and picked up a fork in his right hand and a dull knife in his left. The black man said nothing and sat down one seat over at the counter. The two Arabs sat to the right of big black man.

Ham cut a large bite of his omelet and stuffed it in his mouth. He was hungry and he could tell time was short. He chewed and swallowed. The black man continued glaring as if Ham had killed his dog. Ham noticed the knuckles of his right hand read, *LEROY*. One letter tattooed on each knuckle.

Ham stuffed an entire sausage in his mouth and audibly moaned with pleasure. "*Hmmmm*…that's good sausage."

"What did you say," the black man demanded.

Ham didn't answer. He stuffed a piece of bacon into his mouth.

"I said, what did you say?" the black man was getting angrier. Silence filled the café as everyone suddenly felt the tension. The two cowboys froze and stared. The family was quickly packing up, and no one was arguing. Even the waitress caught her breath as she poured some more coffee in Ham's cup.

"Thanks for the coffee."

The two Arabs coolly observed Ham. Ham noticed the eyes of the leader. Calm and calculating. No emotion.

Ham took a drink of his coffee and then consumed another sausage link. "That is good coffee and good sausage. My compliments to the cook," Ham spoke loudly.

The last Arab to come through the door leaned closer to the leader. "Kafir," he hissed with a sneer on his face staring right at Ham. His eyes settled on Ham's forearm tattoo.

Ham smiled. "That's right. I'm an infidel," Ham said as his gaze penetrated straight into the man's heart. "I speak a little Arabic too." The man looked away and spoke viciously in Arabic to the leader. The leader silenced him by simply raising his right hand.

Ham had had enough. Here he was in the middle of bum-fuck-Egypt-Idaho and he was having a smack down with Arabs. His game face appeared without any muster. He calmly lifted a piece of bacon to his mouth. He chewed demonstrably.

The black man was slightly shaking with anger and anticipation. "Leroy, you alright?" Ham taunted. The man physically jumped at the sound of his name, causing him to almost shout. "My name is not Leroy!"

Ham smiled and pointed to his tattooed hand, "Well, it says Leroy right there. Was Leroy your jailhouse girlfriend?"

Leroy jumped to his feet sending his chair flying behind him. Someone screamed. The waitress dialed 9-1-1.

"My name is Mohammed!"

Ham laughed, "That's fucking original. Did you convert in San Quentin? Hard to fit Mohammed on your knuckles."

"Peace, Mohammed," the leader suddenly spoke and gently lay a hand on Leroy's shoulder.

Ham was no longer thinking of consequences. "Yes, Leroy. Sit. Stay. Be a good boy. Bacon for everyone. I'm buying. You guys should try it. You're missing out."

The veins in Leroy's face were bulging with anger. The leader stared calmly at Ham. "What are you doing here, sir?"

"I was just having breakfast. What are you doing here? Camel races later?"

"Your juvenile insults will not provoke me. I am a man of peace," the leader spoke with a thick Arabic accent.

"No, I guess I can't provoke you, but I don't think Leroy can take it," Ham laughed.

"My name is Mohammed!" Leroy shouted.

Ham doubled his fists as he stood. His weight resting on the balls of his feet. Ready. He'd had enough. He was going to pick a fight now.

"Mohammed was a goat humper," Ham thundered back. His muscles tensed as he could see Leroy was beyond repair. Just one more taunt and…"Leroy, do you like goats? Gotta be careful…I hear they can kick."

"No, Mohammed, peace," the leader spoke sternly to Leroy.

Ham knew he had him. The fire in Ham's belly cried out for blood. His eyes danced as he laughed in Leroy's face and made a goat sound, "Baaaahh!"

Leroy burst forward with a speed uncommon for a man his size. Ham met his charge with fist to the nose. It made a crunching sound as Leroy bulled his way ahead. Blood sprayed down his white shirt buttoned to the top. Ham stepped to the right and let Leroy's body weight do the rest. Ham noticed in a glance that both of the Arabs were standing still off to the side, with no interest of joining in the fight. Obviously, they were used to other men doing their fighting for them.

Leroy was just getting started. He stood up and gathered himself. He wiped his sleeve across his nose and covered it in bright red blood. Leroy twisted his neck popping the joints. He focused his eyes on Ham, "I'm going rip you apart!"

"Whatever, Leroy. You're gonna try," Ham mocked. Leroy stepped in swinging. It was obvious Leroy had no real fight training, which is not uncommon for big men. They often don't fight much. They back most others down with their size, really never learning to fight well.

Ham blocked his flurry and landed a jab to his left eye followed by a left to his nose reopening the wound and sending blood pouring down Leroy's chest.

He stepped back and wiped his other sleeve across his nose. It came back crimson. It was obviously hurting the big man. Leroy charged again. This time he caught a hold of Ham under the left arm pit and drove with his legs pushing Ham entirely backwards as he struggled to get his feet. A shattering sound exploded through the room as they tumbled right through the front window destroying the antique window pane as they went. The two men landed with a thud on the pavement, broken glass all around.

Leroy grabbed a shard of glass and swung it at Ham grazing his right cheek sending blood spraying. Blood ran down Leroy's hand from the sharp edges of the shard he held. Ham ducked backwards just a bit too slow, and Leroy connected solidly to his cheek. Ham's head exploded with pain as he stumbled to regain his footing and fight off the inevitable rush. Ham was hurt, and he knew it. He wished he had a weapon. Instead, he stepped in toe-to-toe with Leroy and exchanged punches. He felt several blows to his face as his knuckles pummeled at Leroy.

"FREEZE!"

Both Ham and Leroy did as commanded and looked up from their fight to see a sheriff with his gun drawn and pointed their way. Ham spit blood from his mouth over a split lip, while Leroy leaned forward putting his hands on his knees, sucking loudly for air.

"Don't move and put your hands up."

Ham shook his head and raised his hands. Leroy went to one knee, but raised his hands. In a matter of seconds Ham was handcuffed.

"You don't have to handcuff me. It was a fair fight. I was just defending myself," Ham protested.

"Doesn't look fair," the sheriff nodded toward Leroy who was now laying on his back as the ambulance showed up.

"Get up, Leroy! You pussy!" Ham yelled.

"That's enough of that," the sheriff said as he pushed Ham's head down into the back seat of his squad car.

Ham noticed the leader come out of the café and stand over Leroy as they sat him up. He shook his head and appeared to be talking to them. The grizzled old sheriff with the star on his chest quickly cuffed Leroy.

"Yes," Ham whispered from the solitude of his hard seat in the back of the patrol car.

A young man with short cropped dark hair and stiff police style hat arrived and quickly placed Leroy in his car. Both officers talked to the waitress and then to Leroy's buddies. Ham could do nothing but sit and watch through the patrol car window. Suddenly, the adrenaline began to wear off. He spit blood on the floor of the car. His head was pounding, and his left eye had gone blurry. He thought if he looked in a mirror his eye would be swelling shut.

"Damn, he hit hard. Well, I gave as good as I got. What the hell...Arabs here....un-fucking-believable. Mac, you missed a good fight."

The sheriff climbed into his car and they drove down what looked like a "Main Street" without a word.

"Looks like a very nice town, sir," Ham offered.

"It used to have a nice café with a nice window 'til some dumbasses fell through it!" the sheriff said with a gruff voice.

"We didn't fall. Leroy drove us both through it. He's strong as a bull, but dumb as a box of rocks."

"I will ask you a question if I want to talk to you," the sheriff added.

"Yes, sir." Ham honored the request and rode on in silence.

After they were checked in to the county jail, Ham's clothes were removed. He enjoyed a thorough search followed with a nice jump suit. He was booked in, and they even got a fantastic mug shot.

"Can I get a copy of that for my scrapbook?" he joked as they took his picture.

Leroy still had some fight left in him. He was screaming at his jailors and fighting as loud sounds of resistance permeated the small headquarters.

Ham was led down several hallways and through a couple secure doorways. He noticed two different large cells. Each one contained only one other person. Both of them were sound asleep on one of the fold-down benches. He was pushed into the cell and the sound of the metal doors slamming triggered a memory. Ham had been locked up one other time, when he was in trouble as a kid back in Texas. It was something he usually tried to forget. The slamming door startled Ham, and he remembered it vividly.

Suddenly, they were escorting Leroy in. "Hey, put him in here with me," Ham taunted.

The sheriff laughed, "I don't think so. I'll run this jail if you don't mind,"

"Yes sir," Ham answered.

Leroy paused long enough to spit through the bars at Ham. The deputy gave him a shove between the shoulder blades. "No more of that."

Leroy immediately found a corner of the cell and went to his knees in prayer. No one bothered him, and Ham sat on a bed and closed his eyes. After a few hours had passed the deputy returned and opened the cell containing Leroy. "Mohammed, c'mon, let's go," he said.

Ham sat up at attention. "His name is Leroy. Where's he going?"'

"His friends posted his bond."

Leroy smiled as he sauntered by Ham still in lockup. "Allah is good. It is good to have friends, huh, Kafir? Where are your friends?"

"I have all the friends I need. Have a nice life, *Leroy*."

"Oh, I'm sure I'll see you again, real soon," Leroy said with an ugly grin. His right eye was completely shut, and he was limping.

"I look forward to it," Ham said and turned away.

Several hours passed and Ham noticed that darkness had fallen over the one rectangular window in the room high up on the opposing wall. The sheriff appeared. He just stared for a moment. "So, you're some kind of war hero or something?"

"If that will mean I can go…then yes, I am," Ham laughed.

"Why were you fighting with that guy?"

"Just because."

"Just because?" the sheriff questioned.

"My big mouth can run, but those guys deserved everything they got. I was just minding my own business, having breakfast."

"Son, you got anybody you can call?"

"No."

"In your stuff, there was a card with the name and number of a woman named Julie. Can you call her?"

"Julie…" he whispered. "No, I can't call her." Ham put his head in his hand.

"You alright son?" the old sheriff asked.

"I'll be fine, but let me tell you, this day started off a whole lot better than it's finishing!"

"Get some rest. I'll let you go tomorrow unless they press charges, but I don't think they will. They don't trust our courts," the sheriff said.

"I will pay the café for the repairs. Tell them I'm sorry. I just couldn't take that Leroy. I'm trying to leave all that behind. I never thought I'd run into crap like that out here."

"No need to apologize. I'm glad you did what you did. Don't tell anyone I said that."

"Thanks. Do you know an old outfitter named Lloyd? That's who I'm looking for."

"Sure do, I can take you to his place in the morning if all goes well. Get some rest. You're gonna have a shiner on that eye."

"I know. It's killing me. I've had one before. I'll see Leroy again."

"You forget about him. He's nothing. You get on with your life. You've paid your dues."

"My life might be back in Boise. I'm on a mission now, and I always see my mission through to the end."

"You make me proud to be an American, son, but you best find your way back to Boise and call that gal. Nothing out here on the river for you but trouble."

"Trouble's my middle name." Ham lay down on the bed. "Tell Lloyd I'm here. Tell him I'm looking for work at the Lost Circus Ranch."

"I'll tell him, but you should think about what I said. Go back to Boise."

"Thanks Sheriff. You're a good man."

CHAPTER 4

RIVER

The sound of metal tapping on metal caused Ham to startle awake and jump to his feet. He blinked quickly to focus his eyes, jaw set, fists clenched. An old man was tapping a lighter against the bars. His hands were weathered with age and use. The knuckles proudly displayed ancient scars of days and fights gone by.

Ham ran his fingers through his dark hair. "It's not nice to wake somebody who's sleeping," he said with a grin.

"Don't I know it? Haven't slept a solid night since 1965," the grizzled old man stated as he sized Ham up. "Sheriff said you're looking for me. Who the hell are you?"

"Good fuckin' question." Ham chuckled, "You can call me Ham. Who are you, old man?"

"I'm Lloyd. That's all, and that's enough."

Ham shook his head. It was pounding.

"Looks like you're not as pretty as you once were," Lloyd said with a smile. "Looks like you took one to the eye."

"I always lead with my face. Pretty as a Ranger is ever gonna be I guess."

"So what are you doing in nowhere Idaho asking for me?"

"I heard you knew how I could find the Lost Circus Ranch."

"You heard right," old Lloyd said with a shake of his head. "What do you want with that place?"

"I'm answering an ad. They need someone to work, I guess. It was my best friend's dream."

"Your best friend's dream? Not yours?"

"Yeah, I'm living the dream here. Locked up with a black eye and a pounding head…if Mac was here I'd kick his ass."

"Mac, your friend?"

"Yeah, what's it to you?"

"Why ain't he here with you?" Lloyd already knew the answer, but he was weighing every word Ham said.

"He fucking died on me. That son-of-a-bitch. Right in my arms. For nothing."

"Gabe."

"Gabe what?" Ham asked.

"Gabe."

Silence grew like a shadow between them.

Lloyd glanced at his feet. "I tried to put his guts back in… but he died right there on the Mekong."

"I'm sorry," Ham said.

"Me too. He was a good friend. Anyway, you and me…we made it home. Now what?" Lloyd asked.

"I don't know. I'm just looking for the Lost Circus Ranch. I already told you. Do you know the way or not?"

Lloyd's icy blue eyes cut into Ham as if he could see into his soul. His face sported a three-day beard that was almost entirely white. His sharp eyes stood apart in his haggard face.

"So are you gonna get me out of here or not?" Ham demanded.

"I guess so," Lloyd said. "Mikey," he hollered. "Come let the kid out. I guess I'll take him."

The sheriff unlocked the cell and stepped aside as he opened the door.

Ham stood and sauntered to freedom. "You might be sorry you did that," Ham said.

"I'm already sorry," Lloyd said with a smile.

"Oh well, there's bigger mistakes you could make," Ham said.

The sheriff motioned for Ham to follow him which he did. Once the paperwork was signed, Ham stepped into a side room and put his clothes back on. Ham followed Lloyd to a deep green 1977 Ford F150. He climbed in. It was old school. Manual windows, a radio, and that was about it. The engine purred like it was new. It was obvious Lloyd knew how to take care of his machine. Ham stared out the window as they drove.

"How do you like our little town?"

"It's perfect. How long you lived here?"

"I came out here after I got back from 'Nam. Been here ever since. Wife died a few years ago. Cancer. Kids moved to Boise for better jobs. I like it out here. It's home. So, why were you fighting with those guys?"

"No reason. They didn't like my breakfast." Ham glanced at Lloyd. "Sausage with a side of bacon."

Lloyd laughed. "That would set 'em off!"

"What the hell are a bunch of those assholes doing here? Farming potatoes?"

"Not farmers. They moved in here a few years ago. They bought an old mining camp and have turned it into some kind of summer camp for new converts."

"A summer camp?"

"The Islamic Council of Idaho sponsored it. They are supposedly peace loving and are just training new converts in the ways of Islam."

"Bullshit, it's a fuckin' training camp," Ham said disgusted. "That guy I fought was an ex-con. They get converted in prison. He's not sitting around a fire cooking up marshmallows."

"It's right next to the Circus. Clyde's had trouble with them."

"The leader of their little group was Middle Eastern. He's not home grown like Leroy. He's from the sandbox. Trouble with them seems to be following me around."

"Sure does," Lloyd said. He pulled into a driveway and shut off the truck. "Here we are. I got to grab some gear and then we can head out."

"We're going right now?"

"Why wait? It's a beautiful day for flying."

"Flying? I thought we would go by boat."

"Why go by boat when you can fly?" Lloyd ambled into the side door of the old ranch style home with Ham following right behind. They were immediately in the kitchen. Ham was stunned at what he noticed lying on the kitchen table. Six semi-auto Glocks with multiple mags for each lay out in a neat row and box after box of ammo.

"You getting ready for an op?" he asked.

"You never know." Lloyd began placing the weapons in a black bag. Once loaded he zipped it shut. "Can you put that in the truck? It's heavy for an old man like me."

Ham shouldered the bag and headed out to the truck. When he re-entered the kitchen, Lloyd was nowhere to be seen. Ham noticed an array of pictures on the wall. A young couple on a beach somewhere with two kids playing in the sand. A high school graduation. Lloyd entered the room carrying a whiskey bottle in each hand, an unlit cigar in his mouth.

"You're a walking commercial for the ATF," Ham laughed and nodded toward a picture of a couple of young men in olive green in a tropical setting. "Is that you?"

"Yep. That's me and Gabe in 'Nam." Lloyd walked right past Ham and out the door. "Let's go."

Ham followed, pulling the door shut. "You want to lock this?"

"No. I don't even have a key for it," Lloyd said as he climbed in the truck. Ham jumped into the passenger seat. Lloyd continued chewing on the cigar as he drove in silence with a determined look on his face.

"What's going on, Lloyd? You look pissed."

"I always look like this. You need anything before we head out? I won't be back for a while, so now's the time."

"I don't know. I got most of what I need in my pack. Was thinking I'd get a new hat. All I have are my boonie and my Ranger cap."

Lloyd pulled into a parking lot and parked. "I'm picking up a load of groceries for Clyde in here." He pointed to a small-town grocery. "You can walk over there and get yourself a hat if you like, but be quick about it." Ham nodded and briskly made his way to the store with a long sign overhead. *Rusty Spur Outfitters.* The heavy wooden door jingled as it closed behind him. A high-school-aged girl looked up from her folding chair. "Hello, can I help you?"

"Looking for a hat," Ham said.

"What kind? They're back here," she said as she led Ham to the back of the store. A wide assortment of cowboy hats lined the wall. His eyes bounced from one to the next. He tried on a traditional straw hat. He frowned. It didn't feel right. He put it back where it belonged. Ham noticed a brown hat made of a canvas material. He put in on. It fit just right. He admired himself in the mirror.

"That one looks good on you," the girl said. Ham had all but forgotten she was standing nearby.

"Yeah, I like it."

"It's also good for the river, because you can crush it into a pack and it won't ruin it. Oh, and the string of course to keep it on your head. It's an Australian Outback hat."

"I'll take it." Ham ripped the tag off of it and left it on his head as he walked to the front and paid the girl.

"You going boating?" she asked.

"No. Working."

"Your eye looks sore," she said with a grimace.

"Yeah, it hurts a little."

"What did you do?"

"Fell." Ham pulled the heavy jingly door.

"Have a good day," the girl said as he left.

"Awful friendly around here," Ham mumbled to himself.

Lloyd slammed the tailgate shut as Ham leaned onto the truck bed. Two large tubs sat in the back of the truck. The lids duct taped on, obviously full of groceries.

"Like my hat?"

"Yeah, that's a humdinger," Lloyd said. "I need one like that." The streets were hopping with activity. People were loading vehicles, and outfitters were flying by with loads of blue rafts.

"Is it always busy like this?"

"All summer long. They come from all over to ride the river." Lloyd turned south. The ground was flat and rugged with an imposing range of mountains to the west. The windows were down and the air smelled of pine. Lloyd turned at the Lemhi County Airport sign and drove to a hangar lot and parked.

A young man with a shock of unruly blonde hair and wearing a mechanics coverall approached them wiping his dirty hands on a rag.

"Lloyd, how's it hanging?"

"Low. You know me."

The young man chuckled, "I sure do. Got her ready to go for you, all fueled up."

"Thanks Charlie," Lloyd said as he clapped the young man on the shoulder. "Can you load these groceries and the black bag?"

"Sure thing. What's in the bag?"

"Nothing."

"Hmmm, figured."

"This is Ham. He's my co-pilot today."

Charlie nodded toward Ham and dropped the tailgate. He grabbed one of the tubs and headed for the hangar. Ham picked up the other one and followed. Charlie loaded his container into the plane. Ham handed him the other one. Lloyd had carried the bag over and handed it to Charlie as well.

"I could've got that," Charlie said.

"I got it," Lloyd answered.

Ham admired the plane. It's green and yellow stripe pattern was crisp and clean. "Beautiful Cessna."

"She's a beaut alright. Purrs like a kitten too. Shall we?" Lloyd climbed in the left seat. Ham climbed in the right.

"Thanks Charlie, see you tomorrow." Lloyd closed the door hard and buckled his seat belt. Ham did the same. Lloyd handed Ham a headset as he put his on.

"Check, one, two, check. Can you hear me, Ham?"

"Check, I can hear you."

Lloyd was busy clicking switches, checking his gauges, and suddenly the engine fired up. Ham felt the plane vibrate with the powerful engine purring just as promised. His pulse quickened. He hadn't been in a small plane like this in a while. The kid named Charlie pulled the wheel chocks and waved goodbye as they taxied out of the hangar and into position.

Ham could hear the conversation between Lloyd and a control tower somewhere. "Cessna four-six-eight, clear for takeoff on the one seven."

"Four-six-eight, roger," Lloyd responded and settled into position with the runway ahead. Ham loved the anticipation. The only thing that would have made things better was for Mac to be sitting third seat. Lloyd pulled on the accelerator and the engine began to roar as their speed increased until the plane lifted off. Ham stared out the window as the scenery that was beautiful from the ground became nothing short of awe inspiring from the air.

"Wow," he said almost to himself.

"Yeah, it's something to behold, ain't it?" Lloyd answered.

"Sure is," Ham said. He could see several rivers winding like snakes across the mountainous landscape. Little blue dots of people in rafts could be seen floating in the river.

"That's the main fork of the Salmon," Lloyd said. "Most of the rafting and commercial activity is there. They let the jet boats on there too."

Wind was buffeting the small plane, causing some adjustments from Lloyd.

"Windy up here," Ham said.

"Naw, this is normal. When it's bad, it's bad. This is a cake walk." Lloyd glanced over at Ham's face. "Don't get sick in my plane."

"I've ridden in a lot worse than this," Ham said. "Where'd you learn to fly?"

"I flew a bird in 'Nam. Air Cavalry. So, when I got home I couldn't stop flying. Seems like I've been flying people around my whole life."

"At least nobody's shooting at you out here," Ham said.

"True enough," Lloyd said.

Ham noticed a camp along the banks of the river. "There's a camp down there?"

"Yeah, it's one of the raft companies. That's Camp Sheridan. Been here for years. Well, they've all been here for years. No new ones are allowed. All of 'em were grandfathered in before it became the Frank Church Wilderness. You can't buy land and build a camp now. Only the old timers grandfathered in have permits. Surrounded by literally millions of acres of public ground. The Church is special...no way around that."

Mile after mile rolled by with nothing. No camps, no towns, just wilderness and the river. Ham felt a peace settling over his heart. He was glad he was doing this...it just felt right. Lloyd descended closer to the river and followed the canyon. He hugged the curves of the terrain like the old fighter pilot that he was. "Look up ahead."

"Another camp?" Ham could see several buildings along the river.

"Your friends," Lloyd said as he turned away from the river and followed a deep canyon.

Well back from the river, Ham noticed a clearing with several cabins along the shear walls in a circle with a central area containing a fire ring and flag pole.

"Lone Wolf Canyon," Lloyd said. "Jihadi central."

Ham laughed. It was only a few miles further and Lloyd ascended and circled around. Ham could see another camp near the river. A main lodge and the rooftops of several other buildings could be seen. Lloyd suddenly descended with an aggressive angle on a straight path down the center of the grass bottom canyon presenting itself as a landing strip of sorts. Sheer walls lined both sides of the canyon. Lloyd focused on his approach while his strong jaw worked his unlit cigar. With a slight bounce, they were on the ground.

Lloyd turned the Cessna and taxied back the way they had come toward the cabins by the river. Lloyd brought the plane to a stop and shut it off. He lay his headset on the seat and climbed out. He reached in and pulled out the black bag.

"Can you hand me the tubs?" Lloyd asked.

"Sure," Ham said and hoisted the heavy tub out the door. Lloyd sat it down in the lush grass. Ham handed him the second one. Lloyd sat down on the top of one of the tubs as Ham grabbed his own pack and climbed out of the plane.

Lloyd squinted toward the buildings. "Here he comes."

Ham could see a man on a white horse approaching while leading another horse. A third animal followed along pulling a cart of some sort. Lloyd smiled as they got closer.

"My friend Clyde and his menagerie," Lloyd hollered.

The man named Clyde brought his horse to a halt. He was slight of build, but looked hardened. His grizzled face could have been carved of stone as his gray eyes settled on Ham. He leveled a stare that Ham was obliged to return.

"My friend Lloyd. What have you brought me? Looks like a lost sheep."

Ham noticed Clyde had a semi-auto sidearm on his hip and a lever action rifle in a scabbard. He looked the part of an old-time cowboy complete with Western-style clothes and a worn cowboy hat on his head. However, the horse was far too dazzling in its beauty, much more than most crow bait cowpuncher's horse, not to mention the pistol should've been a revolver. Times change and stay the same.

"This one here, he came looking for work. Answered the advertisement," Lloyd said.

"What made you bring him out?" Clyde asked.

"He's got sand. You'll see," Lloyd answered.

"He's got a nice shiner," Clyde commented. His voice was low and gravelly.

"Compliments of your neighbors," Lloyd added.

"Really?" Clyde continued to stare at Ham.

"I guess we can see what he's made of?" Clyde said.

"It's been a long time since I went through basic you old coots. I could lick both of you with one hand," Ham interjected a defiant edge to his voice.

"We're not as easy to lick as you think. Old men got nothing to lose you know," Clyde said.

"Everybody's got something to lose," Ham said. "Nice horse."

"It's a Lipizzaner."

Suddenly a dog came zipping up out of a thicket and ran circles around the plane and then jumped its feet up on Lloyd apparently trying to lick him to death. The gray, brown, and black speckled dog had black ears that stood up.

"Blue healer?" Ham asked.

"Mostly," Clyde answered. "She's as smart as they come, Ol' Betsy."

Lloyd was laughing and pushing the dog away, "Betsy get down! Man, she stinks. You should throw her in the river!"

"She gets a bath now and then," Clyde said. A slight smile cracked his hardened face as he looked at the dog. It was not lost on Ham. It was obvious that he loved the dog. Clyde noticed Ham watching and quickly eliminated the smile.

The third animal ambled up next to the plane. Ham was shaking his head incredulously as he admired it. "What the hell is that?" he said as the beast began grazing. It was harnessed and pulled a cart along behind.

"That's Spot," Clyde answered.

"Spot? It has *stripes*?"

The animal appeared buckskin in color, a black mane and tail, with black stripes intermingled all over its body. His ears were large like a mule, and his tail was only about half hair covered.

"Spot is a Zorse," Clyde stated as if he was being bothered by having to explain.

"A what?"

"A Zorse. Half horse, half zebra. Big Jake here that I'm riding is all stud, you see; he'll mount anything with four legs. I used to have half a dozen zebras out here. So, when Big Jake was done with all the Lipizzaner mares, well, he couldn't leave them zebra gals alone," Clyde said with a chuckle.

"You're kidding me," Ham said.

"Nope, Spot is the only Zorse left though. He's the only one with any fight in him. The others were pitiful animals and the fucking cougars loved to eat 'em. I had seven of them for a time. They're sterile. Won't reproduce on their own. That damn lion got a taste for them. Was killin' them as fast as he could eat 'em, but I finally killed that sombitch cat though. Spot's the last of them. I have a zebra mare and one striped stud left, but I haven't seen them all summer either. Got themselves lost in the Church, or they're dinner for another cougar. Maybe you can find them, if you want to be hired on for cowboy work? I'm too old to be riding all over this damn country looking for lost zebras."

"Maybe I could find them. I'm pretty good at finding stuff," Ham said.

"Well that would make Big Jake's day. He misses them sweet striped ladies!"

Ham shook his head. "A Zorse, never heard of such a thing."

"Well, now you've seen one. Load up his cart and let's get some supper on. I'm starving," Lloyd said as he stood to his feet and stretched his back.

Ham loaded the cart behind Spot as Lloyd climbed on the other horse Clyde had brought along. Without a word they started down the trail toward the river, and Spot followed like the good Sherpa that he was.

Ham stood there alone for a moment watching the two old men and their Zorse meander toward the cabin a half mile away.

"Don't mind me fellas, I guess I'll walk," Ham said aloud. He shouldered his pack and followed along on foot. He didn't really mind. The air was crisp, clean, and smelled of pine. He couldn't help but smile as he marched. Anything was better than marching through the desert.

CHAPTER 5

RANCH

The cabin smelled of burning wood. Oil lamps hung on the wall, lighting the rustic room in golden light. The walls, the mantle, even the furniture, was made of roughhewn wood and tanned leather. It was a man place. It reeked of manhood. Ham smiled to himself as he watched the scene like an outsider.

The window past the stone fireplace faced west, and the sun painted the sky a canvas of color as it dropped below the rims of the peaks. The river gurgled, and Betsy worked a large bone near the fire. Temperatures were dropping, and a cool breeze followed the canyon down to the lowest point, which was the river. The two old men sat around a wooden table in the kitchen. Lloyd shuffled a deck of cards while Clyde filled three glasses with whiskey, courtesy of Lloyd's delivery service.

For a moment, Ham heard the repeating sound of small arms fire in the back of his mind. He pushed it out, determined to be present, right here, right now. Lloyd took a solid swig of his whiskey. After swallowing he slapped his barreled chest,

"That's the good stuff. Al Capone's favorite. Templeton rye whiskey, from Iowa."

"Hair of the dog," Clyde added as he handed a glass to Ham.

He raised his glass. "To the river," he stated.

"To the river," Lloyd added. Clinking his glass against Clyde's. They looked at Ham waiting.

"To the river," Ham agreed. After clinking his glass to the others, he swallowed a healthy drink. The fluid entered his mouth and slowly warmed his entire chest. He slid his cup back to Lloyd for a refill.

"Have a seat lad." Lloyd motioned to the empty chair. "Tell us your war stories if you can. Ours are so old, we make most of it up."

"I remember it like it was yesterday," Clyde said without a hint of humor.

"Ahh…I ain't got nothing to tell." Silence waited. Ham took a sip. "It's like any war."

The two old warriors nodded silently.

"The good young men do heroic deeds, and the best of them die far from a home they will never see again. And then some of us…go home, but we always wish we were back there with our brothers," Ham said. A silence lingered after he stopped speaking as everyone held their breath lost in memory.

Finally, Lloyd raised his glass. "To our brothers who never made it home. Maybe they were the lucky ones."

They all enjoyed hearty drinks and slammed their glasses on the table. "You two are fucking philosophers," Clyde growled. "We just tried to kill the damn enemy before he killed us."

Silence lingered for a moment, until Ham and Lloyd both laughed out loud at Clyde's sour way. Their laughter only increased his scowl.

"How did the Lost Circus Ranch come to be? Here you are in the middle of Idaho, with a Zorse and lost zebras?" Ham asked with a lighter tone. A wolf howled off in the distance. Clyde turned his head to listen holding his breath. "He's up on the rim. They know better than to come down to the bottom, usually."

"Tell the boy how you ended up out here a cranky old hermit," Lloyd said with a laugh. His face already red with the warmth of the fire and the whiskey. He stood up and began rummaging through one of the tubs they had brought. "I got you a present in here."

Clyde glanced at Ham and then began picking at his fingernails with a pocket knife, one leg casually placed over the other. "After 'Nam I was angry. Not happy like now," Clyde added a thin smile. That drew a snort from Lloyd who had almost entirely unpacked one tub and moved to the next one looking for his present.

"I hired on at a big spread in Montana. I worked for a good spell, then I met a woman. She was hell-on-wheels, whew-ee, man she was something to look at," Clyde shook his head at the memory. "Well, her husband didn't take too kindly to me... and all my lookin'. I don't know why."

"You did a lot more than look," Lloyd added with a laugh. "Ah...finally, here they are." He produced a fine looking wooden cigar box. Etched into the wood was the imposing image of a rearing stallion adding to the anticipation of the contents. Lloyd placed the cigar box on the table in front of Clyde. Clyde's hands looked far too big to handle the tiny latch, but he managed it, and the lid opened. He leaned in close and inhaled, a smile grew across his lined face.

"They're good, and I thought you'd like the horse motif. Look here...they're named after horses...this one is called the

Appaloosa...here you have this one...the Lipizzaner," Lloyd was like a kid at Christmas.

Clyde took the cigar and smelled it. "Mmm...that's good. Where'd you get these?"

"It's called the internet. If you had a satellite dish out here, you might know. I found them from one of my favorite websites. I just thought you'd like all the horses on the packaging, and they are good cigars to boot."

"No need for the internet out here. I got the river; that's all me and Betsy have ever needed."

Lloyd pulled out a lighter and lit his up. After Clyde trimmed his end with his pocket knife; he lit his as well. Thick smoke wafted around the room.

"You want one Ham?" Lloyd asked.

"Sure, why not."

After he got his going he leaned back in his chair. It felt as if the weight of the world was slowly lifting off of his back. He could hardly believe he had no more missions to go on. Nothing left to recon...no target to take out from a thousand yards...no more battles to fight. Just sit here with these old men, old warriors, smoke cigars, and be alive. The fire crackled as each man stared at his cigar. No one felt obligated to fill the silence with words.

Ham suddenly had a feeling he never felt before. He felt home. The thought of Mac not being present came crashing in like a summer storm. It came so hard he actually jumped in his chair and his hand involuntarily went to his hip in search of his sidearm. Clyde noticed.

"Easy son," he said slowly. "You're home." He poured a little more whiskey into Ham's glass. He smiled as he inhaled on his cigar producing a roiling red circle clouded in a purple haze.

Betsy sat up and pricked her ears to the outside. She trotted to the door and stared at it, whining a bit.

"Need to go out girl?" Clyde said as he opened the door for her. In a flash, she was gone into the darkness. Clyde shut the door and sat down. He noticed the butt on his cigar was at least an inch long and looked to be in no hurry to fall. "Lloyd, nice cigars, big ash. What do I owe you?"

"These can be a birthday present if you like."

"I like. Anyway, after the trouble in Montana, I had to light a shuck. Ended up in Idaho. I heard there was gold still to be had in the right places out here. Thought I might strike it rich. I ran into Carmine Boerio in Riggins at the general store. He was looking for help and I hired on. I've been here ever since."

"Tell him about the circus part. C'mon," Lloyd said as he puffed his cigar.

"Ox had been a Circus man. Ox is what everyone called Carmine. Anyway, he wasn't a big man, they just called him that, I guess I don't really know why. Ox, in his younger days had travelled all over the east coast with some circus. He used to walk the tight rope, juggle, he knew all sorts of tricks, he could stand flat footed and do a back flip and land right on his damn feet," Clyde looked at Lloyd for assurance. "He could still do it when he was seventy-years-old. Unbelievable what he could do really. I worked for him for years. After he left the circus, he bought this place from an old mining company, and really homesteaded it. He got all of his friends to bring him strange creatures, and all manner of odd animals, until he had a real animal circus in the valley. People were starting to float the river and he charged them to camp on the flat by the river, and then he charged them again, to come up and see the animals and a little show. Always a showman, it was really something."

"In 1978 President Carter stopped here and watched the show. Look over there." Clyde nodded to a side wall. "There's a picture of Ox with Carter."

"Carter was a pussy. Damn Iranians had his number," Lloyd said bitterly.

Clyde chuckled, "Lloyd's not over the whole hostage thing. Anyway, I hired on and worked for Ox up until he died. He died out near line shack two, and I buried him in the meadow he liked. He had no family other than his circus friends, so he left the place to me. I've been here ever since. For years, I catered to the rafters, but now I just want to be left alone.

"I'm sick of those granola-eating-bastards shitting on my beach and leaving their garbage everywhere. I don't need their damn money…so they can keep on floating. There are plenty of camps who will take care of them. Hell, most of my exotic animals are gone anyway."

"What did you have other than zebra?" Ham asked.

"Well, we've had some top-notch Lipizzaner's who were trained right. They could dance around, take a bow, do all kinds of tricks. We had a buffalo, but that son-of-a-bitch was nothing but trouble. I was glad the day a griz put him down and ate his liver. We have had eight or nine Longhorn cattle. We had a few African kudu, a couple gemsbok, a bunch of gazelles, we actually still have a few of those in the valley. They're heartier than you think, take care of themselves. The funniest thing is, we still have a few dik-dik out there. I don't know how many. They're wild now, but they've figured out how to survive with the winter and all."

"What's a dik-dik?" Ham asked.

"Tiny little African deer type animal. Two little spikes on its head. Funniest thing you ever saw out in the bush. We used to have some elk and caribou too, but they're all gone now. Ox

58

had a retired circus black bear for a while that could ride a bike, but that was before I came.

"I still have five Lipizzaners. Three of them are trained. Two have foals that we need to take to Riggin or Salmon and sell. I have Spot and Betsy. I have the two missing zebras that you might find. What else do I need?" Clyde chuckled and took another drink.

"Oh, don't forget the pigs. I had four pot-bellied pigs. One kept destroying my garden, so I ate him. The other three, two sows and a boar are MIA. I see their signs, so I know they aren't dead, but they are hiding out somewhere. I think both the sows have a litter, so who knows how many they are now. Anyway, those little bacon-wagons are out there too. I got plans for them, if we can beat the cougars to 'em. We got to round them up."

"What do you mean, *we* got to round them up? So, I'm hired? You got me catching pigs and chasing zebras. You don't have any unicorns, do you?" Ham laughed.

"We did. Big Jake mounted her, and she ran off! Haven't seen her in years!" Clyde and Lloyd laughed loudly. The whiskey was doing its work. Scratching at the door prompted Clyde to lean his chair back on two legs and open it just enough. Betsy ran in and went straight back to her bone by the fire.

After the laughter dissipated, Lloyd slapped his belly. "Goll darn it smells good in here. Are we gonna eat or just drink and smoke?"

"You know where the bowls are," Clyde said without looking up.

Lloyd stood and ambled to the stove. He grabbed three metal bowls from an open shelf and ladled a brown-colored soup into each. He sat one on the table in front of each man. "Where's your damn spoons?"

"Over there, where they always are, you old coot," Clyde answered.

"Ah, I see 'em," Lloyd sat the three spoons on the table and pulled a long loaf of French bread from one of the tubs. He ripped himself a piece and handed the loaf to Clyde.

Clyde followed suit and was soon dunking his bread in the soup. "Dig in Ham."

Ham was suddenly hungry. The soup was a thick beef stew and the bread was fresh. A full belly, some whiskey, and a crackling fire filled him with satisfaction. He helped himself to seconds.

"That's good bread," Clyde said.

"German lady, Obrecht, makes it with an old recipe. Fresh yesterday," Lloyd answered.

After dinner, they settled in comfortable chairs arrayed facing the fire. Betsy hopped up and filled Clyde's lap. He gently stroked her fur.

Each man stared at the embers and gently worked his cigar and whiskey. Sometimes great stretches of silence lingered between comments. No one seemed uncomfortable by the silence.

"How'd you get the shiner," Clyde finally asked.

"I slipped in the shower," Ham laughed. The whiskey was working. "Your neighbors didn't like my breakfast."

"Not surprised. Was it bacon?"

"Yeah, plus this." Ham showed his forearm tattoo to Clyde. "It means "infidel" in Arabic."

"Oh shit, that's funny," Clyde laughed. He rubbed his face with a glance at Lloyd whose head had tilted back slightly, eyes closed, a slight whirring sound with each breath.

"There was one guy, obviously, the leader, then they had a foot soldier with them. An ex-con, a real tough-guy. They convert 'em in prison," Ham added. "Then they bring 'em out here for summer camp."

"Yeah, camp jihad."

"How old was the guy you think was the leader?" Clyde asked.

"Late thirties, tops."

"Gray hair?"

"No. maybe a little, not too much."

"They call him Nasir. He's second. There's an older one, lots of gray in his hair, he's the big boss. They call him Malik."

"How do you know all that?"

"Oh, I've done a little recon. They ain't running no Boy Scout camp neither. You're lucky you just got a shiner."

"They're lucky they're not dead."

"You're a real hard-ass-killer, huh?"

"Yeah, well, not anymore. Now I'm a zebra and pig hunter," Ham said with a wry smile.

"Them damn zebras could be long gone. Cougar snacks," Clyde said. He carefully put out his cigar and stood. He gave Lloyd's outstretched feet a solid kick which startled him awake with a snort. "Go to bed Lloyd."

Lloyd stood without a word and sauntered off down the hall.

"I only got two bedrooms in here, but that couch lays out flat. There's a blanket over there if you need it. Night," Clyde stated as he made his way down the hall.

"Night, sir," Ham answered out of habit.

"Don't need no sir," Clyde said as he disappeared into the dark hall with Betsy following at his heels.

Ham blew out the lanterns, and stretched out his bed. He lay down on his back. Out the window, he could see stars faintly as the moonlight was bright. He stared up at the ceiling. "Thanks for this, Mac," he whispered.

CHAPTER 6

SCOUTING

Ham's blanket was neatly folded on the couch when Clyde ambled into the front room. He knew he hadn't gone far. He fired up the stove, began a pot of coffee, and sizzling some bacon in a large cast iron skillet.

A few minutes later, Ham stepped through the front door. "Smells good," he said.

"Mmmhmm. Sure does. Not liking bacon is some kind of un-American," Clyde concurred.

Lloyd stumbled in and sat down at the kitchen table. Wasn't long until Clyde slid a plate of over easy eggs cooked in bacon grease in front of him. "Thanks Clyde, is the coffee ready?"

"Yep," he said as he filled a coffee-stained formerly white cup with a chipped rim. "Here you go."

"See anybody out there?" Clyde asked.

Ham didn't answer at first as if he didn't realize the question was directed to him. "Nope, just a stunning sunrise and a bunch of water in a hurry to get somewhere."

"Well, we got plenty of that."

"That bunkhouse looks like the windows have been out for a long while. It's making a nice home for critters and birds, but could be cleaned up pretty easy. The other one, the barn?" Ham grimaced. "The roof on a whole section of that thing is about to give in. Still full of hay though. It could be fixed, but it'd take a sight more work than a few days," Ham stated.

Clyde sat down to his own plate. "I never said we'd run out of work."

"No, I guess not," Ham agreed.

"He guesses not," Lloyd laughed.

"Not as much saddle work as I'd hoped."

"Rome wasn't built in a day," Clyde said. "Those buildings have been running themselves down for a while. A little more time won't hurt 'em none. I got saddle work that's pressing if you're up to it?"

"Yeah, that's what I came here for. I'm in if you'll have me."

Clyde lay down his fork and peered over at Lloyd, "What do you think Lloyd? Should I give the boy a chance?"

Lloyd laughed at the joke, "Beggars can't be choosers! Better find him a saddle, before he hops back in my plane and you're out here smoking cigars alone again."

Clyde frowned, "Nothing wrong with being alone."

Lloyd stood and tossed his plate and fork into the wash tub. "Daylights a-burnin'. Better be getting in the air before this beautiful day turns to crap." He slid his jacket on and gathered the two empty tubs while heading for the door.

"Let me get the horses," Clyde said.

"Nah, I could use a light walk this morning. Plus, Spot's standing right out here. He can carry these tubs."

"Alright." Clyde stood and belted on his sidearm. He also grabbed his Henry rifle that was resting in a rack over the door.

"Expecting trouble?" Ham asked.

"I am trouble," Clyde answered.

"Got any for me?"

"Help yourself to Lloyd's black bag." Clyde stepped out into the light letting the screen door slam behind him. Ham immediately rummaged through the black bag on the floor. He clipped a holster to his hip. He picked up one of the brand new Glocks and checked the chamber and magazine. Locked and loaded. He grabbed an extra mag, placed the pistol in its holster, and burst through the door. It felt good to be armed. He'd spent more of the last few years more armed than not. It was second nature and came with a sense of assuredness.

Ham noticed the old men hadn't waited for him and were a few hundred yards down the trail with Spot following right along. Betsy trotted near Clyde, leading the pack. The crisp morning air felt clear and cold in Ham's lungs as he hurried to catch up. It wasn't long before he was walking along with the old friends listening to their banter.

It was obvious they'd been friends for a long time. He wondered if Mac had lived, if they'd been friends over the years like these two. He'd never know.

Clyde and Ham stood and watched as Lloyd readied his Cessna. You could tell he'd done it a thousand times. He did it smoothly and without thought. Years of habit on display. After he had it ready he approached Clyde and stuck out his hand.

They exchanged a firm handshake. "Thanks for the cigars, the food, and the black bag too," Clyde said with a wink. As they dropped their handshake, Clyde tossed a golf ball sized rock into the air. Ham's eyes focused on it in flight. An obtuse shape of golden stone. Lloyd caught it and stared at it in his palm for a moment.

"Thanks, but that's too much," Lloyd said.

"Bring another black bag next time, maybe a couple shotguns. We could do some bird hunting. Oh, and all the hops and sugar you can carry," Clyde said.

"Will do. Not sure when I'll come. I have to go visit the grandkids in Boise."

"No problem, we'll hear ya before we see ya."

"You bet. Thanks Clyde. Ham you take care of that old coot."

Clyde snorted, "I'll be taking care of him."

Lloyd only shook his head with a smile. He climbed in his plane and fired up the engine with the door open. He taxied into position and slammed the door hard. The sound of the engine increased with the beauty of the plane thundering down the grass valley. The sound changed with liftoff, and Lloyd instantly banked left, climbing to safe altitude.

They stood silently watching until the plane was a speck in the sky. His engine could still be heard but he was gone.

"Well, we might as well get some work done," Clyde said. He moseyed down the trail toward the cabin and Ham followed.

Clyde pulled out a whistle that hung on a leather thong and pressed it to his lips to blow. A high-pitched whistle echoed down the valley, but didn't seem very loud.

"What was that?" Ham asked.

"You'll see."

They reached the cabin, and Clyde opened up an exterior door. Ham noticed a small tack room as Clyde grabbed a saddle by the horn. Just then Big Jake and his side kick from the day before cantered into the yard skidding to a halt. Clyde threw his saddle onto Big Jake without attempting to bridle him or tie him up at all. Big Jake stood patiently.

Ham smiled, "He's one of the well-trained ones."

"Yep. Grab a saddle. I ain't gonna saddle your bronc. I thought you were from Texas?"

Ham frowned and grabbed a leather saddle from that tack room. He tossed it up on the other horse. "Who's this guy?"

"That's Sundance. Every bit as good an animal as Big Jake, but not as much with the ladies…gelding," Clyde said with a chuckle.

"That'll do it," Ham raised his eyebrows.

"He don't know what he's missing, so don't feel too bad for him." Clyde handed a bridle to Ham as he took his and bridled Big Jake. "Grab your pack or anything you might want. We won't be back tonight." Clyde disappeared into the house and returned with saddle bags, and another lever action styled rifle. He handed the rifle to Ham. "Here you go. This one's yours."

"Thanks," Ham said. He checked the action and expelled a round while chambering another. He picked up the cartridge from the ground and quickly reloaded it. "Nice gun," Ham said.

"They're the best workin' guns around," Clyde said as he positioned his saddle bags. He slid his lever action into the scabbard, situated his cowboy hat on his head, and mounted. Ham slammed his rifle into its scabbard, grabbed his pack, and they were off. Clyde walked Big Jake for a half mile on the wide trail leaving the cabin. "I'm going to start with a tour of the property today and then we can make a plan tonight. Sound good?"

"Works for me. You're the boss." Ham noticed that the Lipizzaner had a smooth gait and was teeming with pent-up power.

Clyde stayed on a trail that appeared to be winding itself right down the center of the valley. Each side was controlled by imposing cliffs of jagged rock. They passed two different ravines that disappeared into stands of thick pine. Small streams trickled from each ravine bubbling into the main creek that followed the valley floor. The abundance of water made the valley lush and green. Birds flitted in the trees and glimpses of small game bounding into the distance was common.

Clyde reined up. "If you notice all this old fence...that's from Ox. He had the valley fenced and cross-fenced when he was giving animal tours. He kept them in these pens so people could easily see them. They're all down now.

"Next summer maybe, a good project would be to clear it all out. The whole valley is free range, pushing three hundred acres from end-to-end. Only a couple ways down from the rim into the valley. I'll show you the main trail up at the far end. There's a couple other game trails that a horse can't make, but if you're a climber, a human can. There are three line shacks. One in pretty bad shape, the other two are fine. I use them when I don't want to head back to the cabin. Keep your eyes out and you'll see antelope, maybe a dik-dik, if you're lucky," Clyde said and then he abruptly kicked Big Jake into motion trotting off down the trail. Sundance and Spot instinctively followed along.

The valley was stunning. Ham noticed a couple gazelle grazing out in the sea of grass. At first, he thought they were antelope, but then he realized they were more exotic. He couldn't help but smile. This valley was teeming with life and something new and beautiful around every corner.

This place felt like the exact opposite of where he'd been serving the last few years, and he was loving every minute of it. The day wore on and Clyde pulled up and swung his leg over and down to the ground. He stretched his sore back. He pointed to a beautiful pool of crystal clear water surrounded by pines and cottonwoods. "Let's shade up."

Ham smiled at the colloquialism. "Sounds good." He swung down. The men refilled their canteens, and the horses slurped deeply. Trout could easily be seen swimming around in the small oval shaped pond. Clyde sat and leaned up against a massive tree and chewed on some jerky. He tossed a chunk to Ham.

Ham took a bite and chewed. "It's good and salty."

"Made it myself. It's a good batch," Clyde said as he crossed his arms and pulled his hat down over his eyes. Ham stood and walked around the pond looking at the rocky bottom and the beautiful fish in abundance. "Whack!" The sound echoed through the valley, and Ham instinctively stepped sideways and sought cover as he drew his sidearm.

Clyde pushed his hat back on his head and grunted as he stood. He noticed Ham standing with his gun in his hand. "Don't shoot me. It's just a beaver. Damn things startle the crap out of you with their tails. On second thought, shoot the little bastard if you see him. I don't like 'em messing up my creek, and we could make jerky out of him." He gathered Big Jake and climbed aboard. They entered a treed portion of the trail that was fully covered with a canopy of limbs.

Clyde pulled up next to what looked like a mud hole. A scowl hardened his weathered face. "There's a little seep here and those damn hogs have made a waller out of it. I'm gonna have to thin them out, maybe to zero." He didn't wait for Ham to answer and with a click of his heals Big Jake bounded up the slightly inclining trail.

Clyde slowed his pace and peered through the woods. He halted and motioned Ham forward. Once Sundance was parallel with Big Jake, he pointed through the trees. "Right up there, you see him?"

Ham squinted. "Yeah, I see him." A tiny deer-like animal no taller than twelve inches at the shoulder stood defiantly on a rock outcropping. Two little spikes on its head.

"Dik-dik," Clyde said with a smile.

Ham laughed quietly under his breath. The little animal quickly disappeared into the brush.

The trail continued ascending. When they could see the rim, Ham judged they were about half the way to the top. They turned sharply around a bend and suddenly a sheer wall presented itself as an impenetrable barrier. At the base of the rock sat a simple cabin of faded timbers. One door and one window were visible and a simple peaked roof that had grass growing on it, giving it an appearance of being part of the wood itself.

"Welcome to line shack number two. #1 is pretty much gone. I still just call this one *#2*" Clyde said. We'll stay here tonight. The trail up and out is right over there. We'll go up tomorrow."

Clyde trotted Big Jake toward the cabin. He hopped down and quickly stripped the magnificent animal of his gear. Ham did the same with Sundance. The two white animals each took their opportunity and went to the ground for a good roll.

"Glad to have the saddles off," Clyde said. He gently drew his pistol and pushed open the door to the cabin. He cleared the corners and slowly entered. Ham smiled at his caution, but wondered why he did it. What was so dangerous out here? Old habits, perhaps.

Clyde flung open the window and light poured in. He stowed his saddle and quickly lit a fire. It wasn't cold enough to need it, but it provided a welcome feel to the otherwise simple rustic cabin.

Clyde grabbed a couple poles from the corner. He handed one to Ham on his way out the door. "Let's go catch some supper."

It had been a long time since Ham had held a fishing rod and it felt good in his hand. When he was a boy he had fished with a neighbor a few times, with limited success. His dad wasn't the kind to take him fishing.

Clyde followed no trail into the woods, but he was on a mission. About a quarter mile in, the sound of water falling into a pool provided a sweet serenade. The pool looked deep. Worn stone surrounded the small falls and culminated into a large pool damned by beaver. The pond leaked into a creek and wound its way through the trees and down the slope babbling over rocks as it went.

Betsy appeared from the wood and quickly ran to Clyde. He patted her ears. She had some blood on her mouth. "What you been into, Bets?" The dog trotted down to the pool and lapped it up. After her drink, she walked to Ham and dripped water from her mouth while he petted her back.

"She just runs free?" Ham asked.

"She keeps pretty close to me, but she's a free dog, that's for sure. She thinks she owns this valley. If I don't see her for a while, she always comes back."

Clyde readied his pole and tossed his fly into the live part of the stream right where the falls hit the pool. It floated outward and swirled into a more placid section of water.

In a flash and with a tiny splash a trout hit it. "Yes," Clyde exclaimed as he set the hook and quickly began reeling the fish in. Ham's eyes lit up and he tossed out his fly. It didn't land in the right place and didn't drift down stream. He reeled in as Clyde held up the twelve-inch fish he'd caught. "Beautiful, huh?" Clyde asked. It was a dark colored trout with distinct spots and a bright orange splash on its underbelly.

Ham was determined. He tossed his line again. This time it landed more where he had hoped. The fly drifted no more than a few inches when a fish nailed it.

"Ha! Shit! I got one," he hollered with a smile on his face like a ten-year-old.

"They're bitin'," Clyde said as he cast again. In a matter of a half an hour they had eight nice fish.

Clyde was all smiles. "Let's cook 'em. I'm starving."

"Me too."

The sky was lighting on fire with pink, orange, and crimson as the sun set behind the rim. Clyde had the fire right where he wanted it. The fish were gutted and frying in a cast iron pan. Clyde sat by his fire and gently cooked the trout. The cabin had a couple shelves that were modestly stocked with essentials. A huge jug of oil, salt, pepper, a large box of flour, pancake mix, a jug of syrup, and a large container marked garlic season salt. There was another entire shelf full of cans of chicken, tuna, beef stew, and chicken noodle.

"That was the most fun I've ever had fishing," Ham said.

"Yeah, that was good," Clyde agreed.

Clyde pulled his pan from the fire and sat it on the hearth. He grabbed two blue speckled metal plates and two forks. He handed a set to Ham and forked a couple fish onto his plate. He pulled a piece of bread from his pack and tore off a piece handing it to Ham. "It's a feast."

"Only thing we're missing are a couple beers," Ham said with a laugh.

Clyde's eyes lit up like he had a secret. He went to the back of the cabin and pulled back a curtain revealing a small cave of sorts that held a wooden cask on stilts. Clyde took a metal coffee cup and filled it with an amber liquid. He handed a cup to Ham and filled the other one for himself. "We don't go without at the Lost Circus Ranch."

"Where'd you get that?" Ham was incredulous.

"I brew my own. Beer keeps well in a barrel and is good for you. I have a lot to show you," Clyde said as he took a drink and went back to his plate of fish.

Ham took a drink.

"Well, what do ya think?"

"It's good, bitter."

"Yeah, I like the hops."

They ate in silence. The fish were gone in no time. Clyde wiped the pan with his piece of bread, soaking up the leavings.

"Delicious," he added with a sound of contentment. "I love #2. Peaceful out here. Nobody coming or going like down on the river."

"It's pretty awesome," Ham agreed.

Clyde sat his plate on the hearth, and Betsy licked it clean.

"I hope you do more to clean these than let Betsy to 'em?" Ham said as he looked at his plate.

"Yeah, I got some soap and water outside, but they say a dog's mouth is very clean."

"It didn't look too clean earlier. It looked like she'd been eating something dead."

Clyde grabbed his plate and the pan and walked outside. Ham joined him to help. They made quick work of the cleanup and settled into chairs around the fire. They refilled their cups a few times as they talked.

Clyde spread a topographical map out between them.

"See here." He pointed to a spot labeled #2. "We're right there. See the valley?"

Ham's eyes danced over the topo map. He could read a map and enjoyed the detail of this one. Clyde slid his finger down the trail marked with a thin line. "Here's the trail we rode today. Here's the pig bog, here's the main cabin, see here. That is where #1 used to be."

"What's this?" Ham pointed to a small cross.

"That's where I buried old Ox. It's as fine a place to rest your bones as anywhere. You see all the way to the river from there, and there is a nice stand of aspens that shimmer in the wind."

"Sounds nice."

"See here. Tomorrow we'll take the trail the rest of the way out of the main valley. There is a vast high plain up on top and then we do have a second, smaller valley. That's where the rest of the Lipizzaners like to hang out. I want to check on them. Then you can see our border here in the dotted line. Surrounded by national forest for a million acres."

Ham pointed to a dot labeled #3.

"That's the other line shack. It's smaller than this and up on top of the ridge overlooking the other valley. There is a trail, kind of, through the forest that runs all the way to Riggins one way and Salmon the other. No roads for a long ways…only a handful of unincorporated towns mixed in, but even those are a few days ride and they don't have much. Usually, only a few people built some houses or a yurt village and call it a town."

"Where is the summer camp?"

"Right here." He slid his finger. Handwritten on the map it read, Lone Wolf Canyon. "They only have about a hundred acres by the river. It's a smaller valley. It used to be owned by the Swede and his wife. They had a fine homestead they built out of another old mining camp. Raised a family. All their kids left and after the Old Swede died, the kids sold it to these A-rabs. They've been busy ever since."

"Did you name it Lone Wolf Canyon?"

"No, that's what the Swede called it."

"That's funny," Ham said with a smile.

"Why?"

"Because the crazy jihadi's love to train these nut-jobs to go on suicide missions. Either blow themselves up or go off on a shooting spree, Allahu Akbar and all that. They call it a *Lone Wolf* attack. Get why it's funny? Lone wolf attacks…Lone Wolf Canyon?"

Clyde snorted, "I guess it's funny. They're assholes no matter what you call them."

Ham laughed. "I like you Clyde."

Clyde just stared.

"What are they up to in Lone Wolf Canyon?"

"I have some ideas. I'll show you if you stay long enough. You see here. Our valley is only a day's ride from theirs. They've got a couple four-wheelers, which are not allowed out here, but they don't care about our rules. I've found their tracks on the rim, inside my property. I don't care what they're up to, if they'd leave me alone, but I can't abide trespassing."

"What are you gonna do about it?" Ham asked.

"I have an idea to keep 'em out."

CHAPTER 7

SEARCHING

Ham was still sore from yesterday's ride as he settled into the saddle. It'd been a long time since he sat a saddle all day. Clyde and Big Jake were leading them up a winding trail through the ponderosa pines. A light breeze filtered through the woods as cool morning light burst over the eastern rim. They kept going and the trail narrowed to a path so tight that the stirrups scuffed along the sheer walls on both sides.

"Good thing I'm not claustrophobic!" Ham yelled up to Clyde.

Clyde turned his head, "Better not be afraid of heights either for the part coming up."

He wasn't kidding. The sheer walls gave way to a field of shale rock on a steep incline. The trail zigzagged its way across. Sundance stumbled on a rock sending it flying. It tumbled down gaining speed before entirely disappearing off a precipice.

Ham patted his withers, "Easy boy...watch your feet."

Clyde kept moving at a steady pace without stopping or looking back. Ham could see the trees up ahead, only another hundred yards, and they'd be through the shale field. Clyde pulled up once they entered the woods again. He tossed a leg around the saddle horn. "That's the worst of it. Only a couple more miles, and we'll be on the top."

"I didn't like that rocky part. I thought Sundance was going over the cliff with me," Ham said wiping his forehead.

"Bad way to go," Clyde commented. "Best to just give him his head and let him find his own feet." He took a swig of his canteen. "Ready to go?

"Yep."

Clyde kicked his leg back into the stirrup and led off. They exited the trees and found themselves on a large expanse of open ground with scrub brush and stunted pines.

"Wow," Ham said to himself as the view went on for miles in every direction. It felt like the top of the world. Clyde kept on for a couple more hours. The trail began winding downward, and Ham could see treetops below as they were obviously on another canyon rim. Clyde entered a small stand of trees and there sat a small cabin on a rock outcropping with a view dropping off into the canyon below.

"Welcome to #3."

They approached slowly. "Sons-a-bitches," Clyde swore as he looked at the ground. Ham saw the tire tracks he was looking at. Clyde instantly wary, began scanning the area and slipped the thong off his pistol. Ham unsnapped his holster as well releasing his pistol for easy access.

After a time, Clyde swung down and cautiously made his way to the cabin. He entered it with a burst. Empty. Dust flakes floated in the stream of light pouring in from the open door.

Ham followed him inside. It was small. Two beds, a table, and a stove. "Anything missing?" Ham asked.

"Yeah, my good pan and the first aid kit. The kit sits on the shelf right there and the pan should be hanging on that nail by the stove. Good thing I don't keep much here."

Ham stayed out of Clyde's way. His anger was threatening to boil over, and Ham didn't want to be in the way of it.

"C'mon, let's go on down to the bottom. We got time before dark. I want to check on the horses, make sure they're still there."

They mounted and followed an easy trail that turned back on itself to the bottom. A small creek fed the bottom land and it was a mixture of woods and grass fields. Clyde blew his whistle. "These aren't trained as well as Big Jake and Sundance, but they should come."

It wasn't long before three white horses trotted from the tree line. They stopped and whinnied their greeting. Big Jake answered as their ears pricked forward. As they approached Ham noticed that two of them had dark-colored foals running along beside.

"Two foals," Ham said.

"Yep. All of 'em start out that way."

"How can you tell them apart? They all look the same."

"Not once you get to know them. Look at the big one. He's a gelding named Josey. You can tell by the black spot on his withers. The gal to his left is Jane. She's got a visible stripe on her head and is speckled gray. The other one is Oakley, she's the one with a lop ear, some wild mustang bit the tip off it. Don't get attached to the foals. I'm gonna sell them. I don't need any more horseflesh."

"Are you sure Big Jake is the daddy? They're almost black."

"Yeah, they turn white as they get older."

Clyde climbed down and got as close to the foals as he could. They were skittish, but stayed close to their mares who were not going anywhere.

"They're good looking foals. A colt and a filly," he said to himself more than Ham. "They look fine. We can head back to #3."

They rode back up the trail to the rim and #3. They slipped the saddles and bridles off the horses and let them loose. They both kicked up their heels and took off down the trail to be reunited with their friends on the bottom.

Clyde looked more carefully at the tracks as the shadows were lengthening. "Just one four-wheeler."

"Yeah, but two guys," Ham said.

"Yep. You a tracker?"

"A little bit," Ham said as he pointed. "Look, they walked around here. Smoked a cigarette."

"They weren't trying to hide. Tossed the butt right there."

"Have they ever done this before?"

"No. I've seen the four-wheeler tracks before, but never been robbed." Clyde went inside the cabin and had a fire going in the stove in a flash. He handed a bucket to Ham, "Can you go get some water? Out back I've got a catch basin."

Ham took the bucket and stepped into the darkness. He waited for his eyes to adjust. Just enough moonlight made the barrel beside the cabin visible. He lifted the lid and filled the bucket with the clear, soft water.

He closed the door behind him and handed the water to Clyde. He filled a coffee pot with some water and added two dry packets of chicken soup mix. "They didn't take the coffee pot, at least."

"You got a barrel of beer around here somewhere?"

"No, they wouldn't take that anyway."

"Don't be too sure. They're not all as devout as you think. Some will make all kinds of exceptions in the name of jihad," Ham said.

"If those damn A-rabs want a jihad from me, they can have their fill." Clyde was spitting mad.

"Well, before you go declare war…all they've done is snoop around an old cabin and driven on your property a little," Ham was calming.

"And stole my pan and first aid kit. What's next?"

"I'm just saying, you might not want to go off half-cocked."

"I'm half-cocked?" Clyde was incredulous. "How's your eye?"

"It's fine."

"It's still a little yellow. How'd you get that? I'd think you'd be ready to stand up to these A-rab bastards."

"I've had my fill of fighting. I came out here to get away from all that bullshit. Searching these hills for some lost zebras sounds pretty good to me. Let's leave these guys be. They might not bother us anymore."

"I wish that was true, but they're getting more bold every damn month."

"Well…what's the plan?" Ham asked. "Should we march into their camp and demand your fucking pan back?"

Clyde simmered as he leveled a cool stare at Ham. "Fuck the pan, and fuck you." Clyde pulled a stub of cigar out of his pocket and lit it. Smoke swirling around his face. Ham had been around enough tough men to know to when to be quiet.

Finally, Clyde exhaled loudly, "We'll leave it alone, but I don't like it. Tomorrow we can head back to the main canyon. We'll take the horses with us. I don't trust them out here. I want them closer to home. Don't want those A-rabs to get their grimy hands on 'em."

"Sounds good," Ham said as he slurped his soup.

Sunrise found them standing in front of #3. Clyde blew his whistle. As they waited for the horses, Clyde drew his bowie knife from his hip and used it to carve KEEP OUT into the door. Within a half an hour all five of the horses and the two foals came walking into the yard.

Clyde tossed his saddle on Big Jake. Ham did the same with Sundance. The others grazed nearby. They mounted in silence. Each lost in their thoughts. Ham didn't care about Clyde's dour mood; he was having the time of his life. Clyde led off, with Ham following. The other horses fell in line without complaint or lead ropes. When they reached the shale portion of the trail, Clyde reined in. "Don't forget. Just give him his head and sit the saddle. It's a little harder going down."

"Great," Ham said.

Ham could feel Sundance picking his steps carefully. When they finally reached the other side, Ham ventured a look over his shoulder. The other horses followed in single file. The foal's noses bouncing off the tail of their mothers. They all made it across and immediately pressed on, Clyde still stewing in his anger. They paused where the trail left the crevice. Clyde dismounted and slid two long poles across the trail effectively blocking the exit from the valley for the horses.

He quickly mounted and pressed on for #2. They stopped for a snack and to rest the horses. "We can make it back tonight. No reason to stay here. It'll be dark, but we can do it," Clyde added.

"Sounds good," Ham agreed.

Despite Clyde's simmering unrest, Ham felt more alive than ever. Mac was near his thoughts, as if his presence was sharing the experience.

Each hill provided a new vista that was like a dream. The raw beauty was staggering. A fiery sunset sank behind them as they pushed on, with a foggy dusk settling in the valley creating eerie shadows. It was fully dark and a half moon had risen when they stopped in the yard of the cabin, with the sound of the river steady as a cadence as a backdrop. They dismounted and approached the cabin carefully. All was quiet. All was as it should be. Clyde strained to hear anything out of the ordinary. Nothing seemed out of place. He entered the cabin and lit a lantern. Betsy ran over to her spot by the fire and picked up where she'd left off on her bone.

Ham lit a fire in the fireplace as Clyde released the horses. They ate a dinner of bacon and bread.

Clyde finally spoke, "Ox would be twice as angry as me, if he knew those guys had gone into #3. Back in the day, people could have been hung for less."

"Well, what do you want to do? Go over there and pick a fight?"

"No. I'll leave it alone, but when you get back with the zebras, I'm gonna tell you a few more things."

"Why not tell me now?"

"After the zebras."

"Alright, after then."

"I'm going to bed. All that riding wears out my old bones," Clyde said. "Stay up as long as you like. There's a book shelf over there if you're a reader. The bedroom Lloyd had is yours."

"'Night, Clyde."

"See you in the morning. You did good today."

"Thanks, it's beautiful out there," Ham said without moving his gaze from the flames.

"Yep, it's sure something," Clyde agreed as he turned down the hall.

After he was gone, Ham stepped up to the bookshelf. He'd never been much of a reader, but he wasn't tired. Two entire shelves were full of paperback novels with names like *The Sacketts, Flint, The Daybreakers, High Lonesome, The Mountain*

Valley War, and *Mustang Man.* He selected one titled *Where the Long Grass Blows.*

Ham sat near the lantern and let his eyes bounce along the old school typeset and yellowed pages. The cover had a dog-eared corner, but it felt good in his hands. He read until his eyes were burning and his head bobbed. He tossed the book in his pack and made his way to his room. It was small. One double bed and a small chest of drawers left little space for walking and one small window let in a shaft of moonlight. It was perfect, and more than he was used to. Ham blew out the lantern and hit the rack, instantly asleep.

Ham awoke before the sun. He held his breath listening. Nothing sounded wrong. He thought of Julie. Her dark hair hit her shoulders in the moonlight. He wondered if she would even remember him. If what happened meant anything to her at all. Maybe he was just another cowboy passing through? He wished he could call her, but his phone had long since died and there was no service anyway.

The sound of Betsy's toenails clicked on the wood floor as she walked the hall. Ham found Clyde going over the map.

"Morning."

"Morning to you," Ham agreed.

"See here." Clyde pointed to the map with a pencil as he gave his directions. "Head back to #3. Be sure to go down and search the bottom where we found the horses. Those little zebras could be right there, hiding out, and they won't come to no whistle. If you don't see 'em, follow it down and out at the bottom. See this trail here. It leads into a crap-ton of wilderness. I would scan every meadow you see on here. Those zebras like the open spaces better than the woods, but they don't seem to like being up on top too much, so good luck. Watch out for any A-rabs on four-wheelers."

"I will. How long should I keep looking if I don't find 'em?"

"I'd give it a good week. You can hit most all the meadows within reason in that time. If you don't see any stripes after a week, come on back. They're probably cougar bait."

"There's just the two of 'em?"

"Yep, unless they've got a foal."

"How am I supposed to bring 'em back if I find 'em? Do they herd?"

"No, toss a loop around the big mare and lead her. The others will follow. They won't leave her."

Ham nodded.

"I packed your saddle bags with ten MREs, a pound of jerky, a bag of coffee, half a dozen apples, and a thing of spices. If you shoot something big to eat like a deer or elk, you better take what you want and hide the rest under a bush or something. Don't let it be visible from the air. Coyotes and wolves will do the rest. Oh, and I put a bag of sugar cubes in there. That ain't for your coffee. Give one, and only one cube, to Sundance every morning, and he'll be your faithful servant. He's got a sweet tooth.

"Do you want your saddle carbine or you want to sling an AR on your shoulder? I'd take the lever. It'll serve you fine out here. It'll kill any animal or SOB you might run into."

"The lever's fine. I'll feel like the Lone Ranger on my white horse with a cowboy gun."

"Don't fucking think you can call me Tonto. I don't have a mask for you. You better git on if you want to make it to #2 this afternoon."

Clyde walked outside with Ham and Betsy followed. Sundance was grazing in the yard already saddled. Clyde handed Ham the rifle. It was beautiful with the golden metal trademark of a Henry. It felt good in Ham's hand. "I put a box of shells in there too and half a dozen more mags for the sidearm."

"Expect me to be in a gunfight?"

"Never know. I'd hate you to get killed for lack of shooting back," Clyde said with a wry smile.

"Amen to that," Ham agreed.

Clyde slid the bridle on Sundance. "Oh, do you want a tent? I got a small one if you do."

"No. Too closed in for me. I'll take the fly if it's got one."

"Yep." Clyde pulled the fly from the small packaged tent and four stakes. He stuffed them in the top of the saddle bags. Ham tied his own pack behind the saddle and mounted.

Ham pulled his hat down tight on his head. "See you in a week or so. Hopefully with some zebras."

"Good luck."

"You stay out of trouble," Ham said with a wrinkled brow and a smile.

"Me? You're the one riding out into the bush. I'm just gonna hunt me up some hogs while you're gone. Perfect job for an old man."

"Alright. I look forward to pork chops when I get back."

"Git on," Clyde said as he turned to head back into the cabin.

Ham kicked Sundance gently and he was off down the trail that was already becoming familiar.

Ham walked Sundance around the pool they'd stopped at on their first trip. Ham liked to watch the trout swimming lazily about the clear pond. He noticed little sparkles of gold glittering on the bottom.

"Gold," he whispered and shook his head. "Clyde...you're full of secrets."

Ham made it to #2 by early evening. He dismounted and let Sundance go. He was a little worried that without Clyde and his whistle Sundance might not come back in the morning, but Clyde assured him that he would. Hopefully, the sugar cube would do the trick, or he'd have a long walk back to the main cabin.

Ham didn't notice anything out of place. No one had been to the cabin since they'd been there. He grabbed a fishing pole and headed into the woods hoping for some more fish. It was getting dark. The sky was once again a painter's canvas of orange, red, purple, and pink as his fly hit the swirling water.

Almost instantly a huge trout hammered the tiny fly with an aggressive splash. "Yes," Ham cried out fighting the fish in to the shore. The fish was half again as big as any of the ones they'd caught previously. Ham quickly tossed the fly out again. Nothing. Several more casts, and it was starting to get dark in the trees. Ham carried his fish back to the cabin and lit a fire.

The trout was melt in your mouth good. "Beats an MRE," Ham said to himself. He was used to being alone. He liked it even, but he did talk to himself as if he was another person.

After dinner, he spent some time memorizing the map and settled in by the fire with a beer and his book. He wished he wasn't such a slow reader, but he had nothing but time. After a couple more chapters, Ham eased out into the darkness beside the cabin. He stood listening to the night sounds and letting his eyes adjust. A wolf howled up on the ridge, but it felt close. An owl hooted in a tree right by the cabin. Ham smiled at his adventure and thought of Mac as he stretched out on the hard bunk.

He was happily surprised to find Sundance standing in the yard as the eastern rim glowed with the dull white light of the impending sunrise. Ham held a sugar cube in his palm. Sundance muzzled it into his mouth.

"There you go boy," Ham said soothingly. He saddled up and they were on their way as light was filtering through the trees. They made their way through the crevice and across the shale. Ham sat his seat and held his rifle on his lap as he slowly approached #3. It appeared empty.

As Ham got close enough to see the tracks, he could see no one had been there since he'd been there with Clyde. He didn't dismount and turned Sundance onto the trail down into the second canyon.

He came to the spot where they'd found the horses to discover three elk grazing in the tall grass. At the sight of him, they bounded into the tree line. He pushed on with his heart alive. Each crest was a new vision. There was something undeniable about riding a new country. Each sight was fresh and new. Every bend in the trail led to the unknown and excitement seemed to always be over the next hill. This is why he was here.

"Thanks Mac," he whispered. Sundance flicked an ear back listening.

Ham neared what appeared to be the end of the valley as the sun was sinking low. He found a nice stand of pines with a view of a small brook.

"Looks like a good place to camp. Don't you think Sundance?" Sundance shook his head and snorted as if he agreed causing Ham to smile. "Okay then, glad you agree."

Ham dismounted and released Sundance. After a good roll, he began grazing the lush grass nearby. Ham used the rain fly to make a secure place to spend the night. He gathered some wood. Once his fire was going he filled the coffee pot with water and sat it on a rock near the flames. He ate an MRE as fast as he could. It was gone in no time. Old habit. Eating them fast didn't always make them any better, but it definitely didn't make them worse. He chewed on a salty piece of jerky as he slowly stalked the surrounding woods.

The mountain was teeming with wildlife. He saw turkeys, doves, groundhog, squirrels, and half a dozen mule deer. He decided he might shoot a small one if he got the chance. He noticed a line of thunderheads building to the west effectively blocking out the sunset and causing darkness to fall fast and hard. The growling clouds were accented with occasional flashes of white lighting. He eased Sundance back into camp and staked him close. The wind picked up, and the temperature dropped ten degrees in a flash.

"Oh boy, this is gonna be a long night," he said.

Ham slid his wind and water proof jacket on and hunkered down under his shelter. The wind kept howling until about midnight when the lighting and thunder kicked it up a notch, followed by big drops of rain. The fly held and Ham was tucked in dry under it with his gear. The lightning and cracking thunder ruined any notion of sleep. Sundance stood resolute, unphased by the storm with his rear facing the wind. His head would occasionally bob up with a crack of lightning, otherwise he was solid. The storm rolled on in all its fury, until finally, a couple hours passed and as suddenly as it arrived the storm eased on through.

Ham lay back as he noticed stars peeking through the clouds. He'd learned long ago to snag even a few minutes of sleep when he could.

CHAPTER 8

ZEBRAS

Sundance was nuzzling his leg when he sat up. Ham could tell by the stars that sunrise was imminent. Birds had already begun their day as the forest was alive with their music.

"How'd you get loose? You looking for your sugar cube?" Ham rubbed his eyes and rolled to his feet. He handed the white cube to Sundance in an open palm.

"Dude, you're an addict," he laughed as he patted his neck and popped a cube into his own mouth. The day rose fresh and sparkling after the storm. Water dripped from the leaves as Ham glanced at the map and mounted Sundance. The saddle felt good.

At the end of the second canyon, a thin game trail led through another steeply descending crevice to open to yet another canyon. On the map, Ham noticed a series of four canyons before the elevations opened to a wide valley that extended for miles with a range of peaks along the west edge. The series of canyons turned a little east by southeast and essentially wrapped around the property that was marked on the map as Lone Wolf Canyon.

Clyde had drawn the locations of several cabins in with black pen. A few miles of rough country separated him from Lone Wolf Canyon. He planned to leave them well enough alone. "Live and let live, right Sundance?" Ham said as he tucked the map back into his coat pocket. Sundance only offered a flick of the ear in response. By midday he'd entered the fourth canyon.

Each canyon was similar, yet somehow unique. A group of half a dozen muleys stepped into the clearing and began grazing. They were oblivious to Ham sitting his seat in the tree line. Heads down they grazed on the lush grass along the small creek zigzagging its way to the south end of the canyon. Ham noticed one buck, several mature does, and a smaller doe, probably a yearling.

He slid his rifle from its scabbard. He settled it to his shoulder and exhaled as he centered the open sights on the shoulder of the yearling. His trigger finger slowly tightened.

Boom! Boom! Boom! Boom!

Sundance startled as a serious of shots rang out from just down the valley. The mule deer bolted into the trees and Ham focused his attention as more shots rang out in quick succession.

"Semi...big caliber..." he whispered as he dismounted.

Ham tied Sundance securely, checked his pistol to be sure all was as it should be. Locked and loaded. He replaced it in its holster and eased into the woods with the rifle in his hands. Like a ghost, he moved toward the sounds. He could hear an engine running and voices. The shooting had stopped.

He found a spot under a pine tree with a view of the end of the valley. He could see two men standing near a four-wheeler. He put his binoculars to his eyes and could see what they were doing.

"Son-of-a-bitch," he swore bitterly.

One man was on his knees working over an animal they had downed. The standing man grabbed a leg and rolled the carcass over as the other man cut the remaining tissue. They cheered as the man on his knees stood and tossed the hide over the back end of the four-wheeler. It was black and white striped.

"Clyde's gonna go ape-shit when he hears this," Ham said to himself. "Oh no."

Ham noticed the men weren't done. They walked over to a second animal and began working on it. He could see its legs were also striped.

"Killed both of 'em. Bastards."

Ham eased from his position to get a closer look. In his mind, calculating what he should do. He could kill them now and save Clyde the trouble. Somehow, he knew he wasn't going to kill these guys over a couple of poached zebras. He just wanted to get closer to get a better look at their faces. Ham raised his binocs again. Out of the corner of his eye, he caught a glint of sunlight on a barrel. Instinctively, he jerked his head back. Blinding pain was followed by darkness.

It was dark when Ham opened his eyes. His hand immediately went to his head as a dull pain ripped through his foggy consciousness. His fingers gingerly assessed the wound as the moon rose from behind a peak. He could feel a nasty gash that ran from his right temple and passed the top of his ear. Blood had dried all over his face, neck, and shirt, and it felt like the wound was still seeping. His right eye was swollen almost shut and his entire head was pounding. He sat motionless, listening. Nothing abnormal. His rifle lay on the ground beside him. He quickly picked it up and chambered a fresh round, easing the hammer down to safe. Obviously, whoever shot him had left him for dead and had not bothered to approach his body.

"They hightailed, I guess. Good thing I'm hard to kill."

Ham stood and tried to clear his head. He was dizzy and thought he probably had a concussion. The moon filled the valley with a blue light. Ham could see the carcasses, but no sign of the men, and the four-wheeler was gone. He stepped from the trees and made his way toward what remained of the zebras. He stared down at them. One of them had been partially butchered. Both had given up their hides and heads.

"Assholes. Clyde was right. So much for live and let live."

Suddenly a bleating sound emanated from directly behind Ham. He wasn't thinking too clearly and was angry he hadn't been more alert as he turned quickly, dropped to one knee, and raised the rifle to fire. Stumbling toward him from the brush appeared a baby zebra.

"Fuck me," Ham swore lowering his rifle while enduring the pain of reopening his head wound.

The little striped horse walked right up to him as if it was a tame dog. "What do you want?"

The little thing was shaking. Ham glanced at the carcasses. He quickly found a sugar cube and offered it to the baby zebra. In a chomp, it was gone.

"Sundance is not going to like to share those. What the hell am I gonna do with you?" Ham talked to himself. He considered just shooting the poor little orphan and even raised his rifle. He knew he couldn't do it. The little thing was nothing more than cougar bait out here, and he was too big to carry. Ham's pounding head reminded him that his first aid pack was back with Sundance, so he started marching. In his state, the marching looked more like staggering.

"Good luck, little Stripey. Sorry about your folks. Life's a bitch sometimes." He turned and noticed the little zebra standing between the carcasses. "He won't last the night," Ham said as he kept walking. He made it about half way back to the tree line when suddenly Stripey appeared at his side.

Ham paused and gave him a look. "Good choice. If you want to live, you better keep up little guy."

Sundance snickered as they approached. He'd been tied up a long time. Ham walked him to the creek and let him drink as he applied ointment to his wound and attempted a bandage. The wound was difficult to work with and Ham was groggy. He used an ankle wrap to go around his entire head and hold gauze in place. He noticed his hat had a hole in it from the bullet as he stuffed it into his pack.

He lay back right there by the creek and slept. It was a fitful sleep, but he felt a little better as he climbed aboard Sundance in the crisp morning light. Sundance acted like he knew the way, and Ham rocked in the saddle in and out of a painful fog. Stripey kept up and followed right at Sundance's side. Dusk was settling on them as Sundance stopped in the yard of #3.

Ham half-dismounted, half-fell from the saddle. He stripped the bridle and saddle from Sundance, letting it lie right where it fell as he stumbled to the back of the cabin and drank deeply from the water barrel. He leaned his full weight on the rim of the barrel and splashed his face with the cool water. Ham's right eye was nothing but a swollen crease, which didn't help with his depth perception. Darkness fell as he swallowed his last sweet drink. His stomach loudly complaining from lack of attention. No moon left the side of the cabin dark. He stumbled around to the front and found his flashlight in his pack. He dragged the pack behind him as he pushed open the cabin door.

He opened a can of peaches that looked like it had been on the shelf for some time. He scarfed down the peaches and hungrily drank the juice letting it spill down his chin. He was still dizzy and sprawled out on what passed for a bed in the corner instantly asleep.

Throbbing pain woke him. He sat up and put his hand to his wound. Light was streaming in the door of the cabin he hadn't bothered to close. Both Sundance and Stripey stood in the door looking at him with their ears pricked forward as if to ask, "Are you alive in there?"

Ham chuckled. "You guys miss me? Or just want your sugar?"

He felt more pain than dizziness as he stood. He was glad for that. He sat at the table and propped up a mirror to have a look at the wound. The outer wrap came off easily, the gauze was stuck tight to the wound with dried blood and scabbing.

He tugged at it gently. It refused to come off. "Damn," Ham swore. He knew it was gonna hurt like hell to pull it off. He grabbed the bucket and filled it with water. He squinted his one good eye against the bright sunlight and was glad once he was back in the dark cabin. He used a rag to soak the wound for a few minutes with the cool water. Then he tried at the gauze again. It came free a little on the corner. Encouraged, he soaked it longer with the water. After repeating the process several times, he gingerly removed the gauze to reveal the wound.

It was deep and raw, like a half-inch-wide furrow clear to the bone. "The bullet bounced off your hard head," he said to himself. The edges of the wound were red and puffy. He tried to push it together. There wasn't enough skin remaining to bring the edges together for stitching. He couldn't decide if that was a good thing or not. The idea of trying to stitch it gave him the shivers up his back.

"You're not gonna be as pretty after this heals up ugly," he said. "You never were that pretty," he answered himself. "It'll be a good scar, if you don't die from it out here."

He decided to reapply the ointment and keep it covered. That's all he could do. This time his bandage was much better than the one he'd rigged in the blindness of the field. The sun was sinking in the west; he decided to stay the night and in the morning, he would make for Clyde's cabin.

"I can't wait to hear what he has to say about this," he said with a chuckle imagining a barrage of swearing. There was enough wood in the cabin for a fire. Ham heated water, mixing in a packet of chicken soup. It was delicious. He drank down the broth and sat back near the fire enjoying a full stomach, his head still pounding. He boiled a pot of coffee. Once he had a cup he sipped it as he recounted what he'd seen, attempting to burn it to memory, as everything since getting shot had been a bit foggy.

He could remember the faces of the two men. Both were dark and bearded, like he'd seen a thousand times before in the Middle East. He was sure he'd seen neither of them before. "I'll see you again, though, and soon," he whispered, thoughts of retribution driving him on. The four-wheeler was red. That was all he could remember.

He took another sip of his coffee. It was strong, just like he liked it. "If you hadn't thrown your head back, you'd be dead out there on the ground." He always talked to himself as if he was someone else. "Mac, what have you gotten me into?" He lay back down on the bed. Dark dreams startled him awake more than once throughout the night. It was the kind of night that never seems to end, but somehow, they always do.

The sun rose clear and strong bursting rays of light over the rim announcing its arrival.

Ham staggered to the yard and gave Sundance his sugar cube. In exchange, he stood still as Ham heaved the saddle onto his back. His equilibrium was still off as the dizziness returned with any kind of exertion. He managed to tack up, but slowly. He closed up the cabin and climbed into the saddle.

He had to stop frequently and sip water and rest. He realized he was only going to make it to #2 before nightfall and not all the way back to Clyde's.

"Oh well, maybe I can catch a couple fish for supper," he said to Sundance, only garnering the usual ear flick. As they crossed the shale, Stripey lost his footing and started to slide. His little hooves made a clickety-clackety sound as he scampered across the shale moving beneath him. He was all legs, but somehow managed to reach the firm part of the trail with only his front two knees slightly bleeding from the falls.

"You're lucky to be alive Stripey," Ham said as they headed into the crevice trail. Stripey kept close to Sundance. It was midafternoon when the rooftop of #2 came into view. It felt good to be on the ground. Aside from being hungry, Ham was feeling tenfold better. He'd tried the jerky, but it made his head pound to chew that hard. He found he could suck on it and get the flavor at least. He quickly grabbed a fishing pole and headed for the secret spot.

Four trout later, Ham was back at the cabin with a fire going. He used the hot water to clean his wound. It had a sort of scab, but still looked angry and was too sensitive to touch. Even cleaning it and applying the ointment was all that he could bear. The fish dinner was a succulent reward. His right eye was black and swollen but he could see a little more than the day before.

Ham lay the map out on the table and marked a red X in the middle of the fourth valley. He labeled it "Zebras Killed." He analyzed the topography and determined where the likely trail would be from the Zebras Killed location back to Lone Wolf Canyon. He imagined the men feasting on zebra steaks and laughing about him being bear bait, dead out in the middle of nowhere. Anger slowly percolated throughout his being. He was feeling better, and their time would come.

He lay his weapons out on the table. With a rag and some oil, he lovingly cleaned them all. Preparing them for what they were made for. He would be ready. He wouldn't allow them to surprise him again.

CHAPTER 9

HOGS

Clyde watched Ham go until he turned down the trail into the trees and was out of sight. He saddled up Big Jake and hooked Spot up to his cart. He grabbed a box of shells and slammed his rifle into its scabbard, "Let's go shoot some bacon!"

He climbed aboard. It was harder than it used to be, but he would die without complaint. He winced at the pain in his joints and pushed through the fear that he was getting weaker all the time. Big Jake stood patiently, the picture of power, muscles taut under a shimmering white hide. Clyde kicked his heals, and they were off. He tossed Betsy a small piece of jerky as she trotted along, never far from his side, always faithful.

By noon they'd found the seep where the hogs liked to hang out. Clyde dismounted and picketed Big Jake. Spot wasn't going anywhere without Big Jake, no need to picket him.

Clyde found a spot in the trees; he'd been there before. He knew this valley like the back of his hand. He'd made it his life.

He settled atop a nice rock outcropping with a good look at the hog wallow. He lay his lever across his knees and began to chew on a chunk of bread he'd brought along. Betsy lay down beside Clyde. He gently patted her coat. It was a beautiful day. It didn't bother Clyde to have no one to share it with. He was used to being alone, other than Betsy and Big Jake of course. He wouldn't have it any other way.

He thought of Ham riding off looking for the lost zebras. He did like the new kid though. "He reminds me of me," Clyde said as he talked to himself. Betsy raised her head as if he'd been talking to her. Clyde scratched her ear. She leaned into it.

Suddenly, half-a-dozen hogs appeared in the field. Shaggy black beasts with pot bellies. Snorting and grunting all the way to the seep. It didn't take long, and they were all laying in the mud enjoying the cool dampness. Clyde's sights settled on the lead sow. Boom! The rifle leapt in his hand, and the sow took the bullet between the eyes. With a *woof* the other hogs jumped to their feet, but they didn't know what was going on so they just stood there looking at the dead sow.

Boom! A smaller sow with eight piglets took a round through her earhole. She dropped with a thud. Another shot and the boar was dead too. Finally, the remaining hogs took off running for the trees. Clyde rolled one of them with a shot to the shoulder. The other two were hot-footing it as fast as their short legs would carry and they made it to trees.

Clyde was laughing out loud, "Pork chops for dinner! Woo hoo! Got 'em!" He hopped up from his seat and led Big Jake to the hogs. Spot followed along. Clyde quickly set about his work. He had plans for these hogs beyond a fine barbeque. Clyde discovered all the piglets still suckling on their dead sow. They were small and he quickly dispatched them one at a time with a hammer blow to the back of each head. He didn't feel bad about it. It was just part of the job.

"They multiply like rats. Too bad I didn't get 'em all," he said as he tossed the little pigs into the back of Spot's cart. He butchered out as much meat as he could keep and then removed the heads and feet of the other hogs loading it all into the cart. He chuckled as he worked, thinking himself quite clever.

He mounted Big Jake and followed the trail up to the rim that separated his property from Lone Wolf Canyon. He pulled up short when he noticed tire tracks from a four-wheeler. He scowled at them and dismounted. He grabbed his hammer and nails and one of the dead piglets. He nailed the piglet to a tree that would be easy to see. Then he took a sign from the cart that was premade. He nailed it below the pig. It read—*Keep Out! Private Property! This trail covered in pig blood!*

He admired his work. With a nod, he kept on. He placed all the dead pigs along the trail, each with their own sign. Clyde evenly spaced them about a quarter mile apart. He was disgusted by the obvious use of the trail by their four-wheelers. This ridge was well within his property. It wasn't even close, so there was no mistaking it. Clyde discovered several locations where there was lots of foot traffic. Each spot had a good view of the valley below. One in particular had a clear shot of the main cabin and river.

"Watching me, are ya? Bastards," Clyde said as he took one of the large hog's heads out and hung it directly above the vantage point that looked at the cabin. He continued on his mission and hung several pigs' feet as well. "This'll teach you to spy on an old man," he mumbled. Betsy cocked her head as if he was talking to her. She trotted off down the trail, never getting too far away. When she was younger she would disappear for days, but she stayed pretty close now as her spry years were a distant memory.

Big Jake crested a rise in the trail, and there it was. Sitting like a new bike on Christmas morning. A blue four-wheeler sat right in the middle of the trail. Clyde brought Jake to a halt, instantly aware.

"You sons-a-bitches," Clyde said at the sight of it.

No one seemed to be around. Clyde held his breath listening intently. He couldn't hear as well as he used to, but he heard nothing. He glanced side-to-side. He slowly eased Big Jake forward. He reached the four-wheeler. He sat his seat listening. Still nothing. The sight of it pissed Clyde off. He had a thought...he couldn't resist.

He climbed down and went straight to the four-wheeler. The keys were in it, but he didn't start it. He didn't want to draw attention to his discovery. Clyde grabbed the keys and was about ready to toss them into the brush when he noticed the four-wheeler sat on a slight downhill incline. He chuckled and put the keys back in the ignition. He climbed aboard and popped it into neutral. Gravity took over and the four-wheeler began to roll. It took all of Clyde's strength to steer it. He saw his target just up ahead on the right, a steep ravine dropped off quickly, it was more than a hundred feet into the rocks and brush below.

The four-wheeler began picking up speed. Clyde's face showed the fear of his wild ride as the four-wheeler hit a root and then rock. At the last second, Clyde turned the ATV into the ravine and bailed out. He bounced and skidded along the gravel and sat up in time to see the four-wheeler disappear into the ravine. Blood ran down his face from a scuff on his forehead, and his elbow was also a scratched and bloody mess.

None of that bothered Clyde as he laughed at the sight of the four-wheeler crashing to the bottom. He struggled to contain his laughter. He dropped a pig foot right in the trail and climbed aboard Big Jake hurriedly heading for the safety of his canyon. He kept a watch behind, but never did see or hear anyone. He continued to laugh at his mischievousness as he made his way to the cabin. It had been a good day. It was dark before he turned Big Jake loose and headed into the main cabin.

Clyde settled in next to the fire and tossed Betsy a biscuit. She swallowed it in two bites. He pulled out a worn leather book with a wraparound leather latch. It was old and worn from use. Clyde thumbed through it until he reached a blank page. He quickly wrote the date and then titled the entry: *Hogs and a Four-wheeler.*

He then proceeded to write out the details of the day's events in a matter-of-fact journal format. When he was done, he sat the journal on the table and leaned back in his chair. He listened to the sounds he knew by heart. He could hear the river first and foremost, but beyond that, much more...an owl who loved the old barn screeched, a smack of a beaver tail was no surprise, each night sound had its place. Clyde exhaled deeply. He was tired. He knew his time was getting short. With no family, what was to become of this place? He suddenly understood what old Ox had been going through when he left this place to him.

Clyde opened the journal and titled a new page and dated it.

Last Will and Testament. To whom it may concern. I, Clyde Hawkins, of sound mind, upon my death or serious maiming where I can't get around no more, do hereby give the entire control and ownership of the Lost Circus Ranch on The River of No Return, Idaho to the man named Lance Hamilton. IF he is dead or maimed, give it to my friend Lloyd Jenkins of Salmon, ID. He is old, but he can give it to someone of his choosing. Thank you. I am dead.

And by God don't let those SOBs from Lone Wolf Canyon ever buy it, or I will haunt you forever. Signed and dated. Clyde Hawkins.

Clyde lay the journal on the table and stirred the fire. He picked up his glass of whiskey and raised it to Betsy. "Well, there it is then. The kid doesn't know it yet, but he's just inherited a gold mine." Clyde grunted as he heaved himself to standing and sauntered outside, Betsy at his heal. He walked down the trail to the river and settled into an old wooden chair that was threatening to fall apart. The moonlight lit up the night, bathing everything in cool gray light.

The old chair creaked under his weight. Clyde remembered the day he'd built it with Lloyd. They'd sat here by the river in their newly built chairs, drank whiskey, and smoked cigars while the rafts floated by.

He remembered part of that day vividly. A young blonde woman had seen them sitting in their chairs, and as she floated by she took off her bikini top and shook what the good Lord gave her. Everyone in the boat was laughing loudly as he and Lloyd had jumped to their feet and cheered.

"Heck, that's been twenty years ago," Clyde said to his memory. "That gal is fifty years old somewhere by now. Bet she don't look like that no more!" He took another sip of his whiskey. "None of us look like that no more."

The river was beautiful in the wondrous light. Divine even. He loved this place. Clyde slowly ambled back to the cabin with Betsy by his side. Her ears jumped to attention, and she growled low as a cougar screeched out across the river. "Easy girl, that lion won't bother us," Clyde said as he dropped the latch on the door to the cabin behind them. He made sure the fire was contained and found his bed.

Sleep came easy, it didn't stay easy. Clyde was happy to get a good, solid four or five hours before he either had a dream that startled him awake or he had to relieve his bladder. Either one meant it was much harder to get back to sleep and usually meant he was up. Maybe it was his age, but in those quiet morning hours he found himself, more often than not, pondering the hereafter.

He had never been an overly spiritual man, but as he neared the end it seemed to be of more importance. Clyde would read the good book while sitting close to the fire. He was surprised that he found comfort there. Other times he leaned back in his chair, and it put him to a peaceful sleep.

Sunrise found Clyde down by the river with a notepad. Once Ham got back, zebras or not, he meant to put his young muscles to work. He started a list.

Repair roof of barn
Rebuild corral by barn
Clean out old barn
Tear out old fences (Next year)
Build new fences
Clean up junk behind barn
Chop firewood

"That's a good start. Firewood should be number one, and there's a lot more than that, but if we even got some of that done, it would be good…before winter sets in," Clyde said to himself as he looked at the list.

The sound of a fast boat edged out the silence and caused a furrow and a squint to come across Clyde's face. He tucked his list into his shirt pocket. The shiny silver and white jet boat appeared around the bend and quickly landed itself on the sand. Clyde noticed his rifle leaning against his old chair twenty feet away. Several dark men jumped from the boat and quickly made their way toward him. Clyde started toward the rifle. He didn't make it.

The man he knew as Nasir stepped between him and his rifle with a smile from ear-to-ear. Nasir picked up his Henry, "You looking for this old man?" Nasir appreciated the gold plating. "Nice cowboy gun. Are you a cowboy?"

Clyde set his jaw and glared. He noticed an older man approaching in the middle and a younger man quartering on his left. Clyde knew he was in trouble.

"What can I do for you, gentlemen? Wasn't expecting company? If I'd known you were coming, I'd have cooked up some bacon," Clyde called out with a wry smile across his grizzled old face.

The older man with a little gray in his beard approached with his head shaking side-to-side as if in frustration. "I don't believe we've officially met," he said, his English thick with an Arabic accent. "My name is Malik al…"

"What the fuck do you want? The sign on the beach says private property…keep the fuck out!" Clyde interrupted him.

"No need to be hostile. We are neighbors. Are we not?

"Can't pick your neighbors I guess," Clyde continued.

"That is true, very true, but this is the land of the free, correct?"

"That's right. Bought and paid for with the soldiers' blood."

"Ah yes, the soldiers' blood. Hmm…yes…it pays for everything. I agree. In my homeland, we understand that.

Maybe you can help us out. You see, we're missing a four-wheeler…an ATV?"

"ATVs are illegal in The Church. Why would you have one out here anyway?"

"Well, it was a gift, and it is missing…do you know what may have happened to it?" Malik said with a knowing look to his face. It was obvious he was playing a fool.

"Quit fucking around. Somehow, it fell into a damn ravine, because you assholes kept driving it on my ridge. Now get the hell off my property! I don't need any neighbors or friends. I like to be left alone!"

"You are definitely alone," the man on Clyde's right spoke.

"Who the hell are you?" Clyde snapped.

"This young man is a member of our camp. Training in the ways of truth, to serve Allah," Malik answered for him.

Clyde guessed he was the fellow who had tangled with Ham in town. He looked the part.

"So, you're just a summer camper? A real fucking Boy Scout, huh? Bet you aren't learning how to tie knots or start a fire in the rain. You're the one they converted in the pen, aren't you? What'd you get sent away for?"

The man glared with a sick smile and nodded silently.

Clyde was angry, and he'd never really learned how to hide that. "You guys pray like ten times a day, right?"

"We honor Allah five times a day with Salat," the man replied with an arrogant sneer.

"So those callouses on your knees from all that time in the pen must come in handy for you!" Clyde said with a laugh. The man took a step toward Clyde his face dark with rage.

Malik raised a hand to stop him.

"It must be hard to live out here all alone like this?" Malik continued.

"You get used to it," Clyde said.

"So many dangers. An old man could fall in the river and drown. He could get bucked from a horse and break his neck. His cabin could burn down, and he could even go crazy and shoot himself in the head," Malik said with a slow method to his speech.

"Well, I'm not entirely alone," Clyde said.

Nasir laughed out loud. He began working the lever action unloading the shells onto the ground.

"Stop that," Clyde protested. Nasir didn't stop until the rifle was empty.

"You see, you are alone," Malik added.

"My man will be back soon," Clyde retorted.

Malik shook his head no. "I wouldn't count on that. You see, I was trained in Africa, and I acquired a real taste for the exotic. Especially...zebra, oh my...prepared the correct way, zebra is an absolute delicacy," Malik said as he pulled a piece of striped hide from his pocket.

"You bastard! You killed one of my zebras?" Clyde said.

"Your zebra? Who can say whose zebra is whose? They all look alike...do they not?"

All three of the men laughed at that. "Yes, and I don't think your man is coming back...ever," Malik said. "It's quite dangerous out there. A million ways even a young man can die."

Clyde knew he was in real trouble. Betsy leaned up against his leg and growled. "He'll be back."

"I'm not here to quibble about four-wheelers or even zebras. I am a reasonable man. I am here to make you an offer."

"Shove it up your ass Mohammed!" Clyde had had enough.

"My name is Malik, and usually you must hear the offer before you reject it so violently."

"I will pay you fair market value for your property...in cash...if you will sign it over and leave within one week. I just think it's for the best. Like I said, it is *very* dangerous out here for an old man," Malik said with a malicious smile.

"Thanks for the offer, but shove it up your fucking raghead ass!"

"I was afraid you would say something eloquent like that," Malik nodded at his seconds and turned toward the boat. He paused with a look back, "You have three days to say yes. Two days to think, and on the third day we will return with a contract for you to sign, then I'm even giving you some days to pack up and go as a token of my generosity."

"Go fuck yourse…"

"Oh yes, go fuck myself, very original…you have two days to come to your senses. I would appreciate less vulgar talk when you accept my generous offer. You can be a wealthy old man and live out your days in Boise."

"If you bring a contract…I will wipe my ass with it! Keep off my property!"

"So, tough. So, brave. My friends will show you that if you don't accept…like I said, things can be very dangerous out here."

Nasir stepped toward Clyde with his fist clenched at his side. Clyde began coughing and leaned forward as if in a fit. With no warning, Clyde launched an upper cut right to Nasir's chin. Nasir didn't see it coming, and he hit the ground hard. He wiped his mouth with the back of his hand. His anger flared as he spit blood.

The other man viciously hit Clyde in the back of the head with a closed fist sending him to the sand with a thud. Nasir stood and stepped in close with a vicious kick to Clyde's head. Clyde pulled back at the last second causing it to be only a glancing blow. Clyde tried to jump to his feet, but he wasn't fast enough to avoid a kick from the second man to the ribs. He felt an explosion of pain as the wind was knocked out of him. At the same moment, Nasir punched hard down onto Clyde's right eyebrow splitting the skin and spraying blood.

Clyde's head spun and he felt sick. He fell back and Nasir straddled him, rolling him onto his back, pounding his face repeatedly. Clyde lost all real consciousness as he put his hands up in an attempt to block the blows. Suddenly, the barrage stopped. Clyde rolled onto his stomach and rose to his knees. His right eye was already swelling shut and a yellow hue from the blood in his eyes altered what vision he had left.

"No," he cried out as he saw Nasir carrying Betsy. She was struggling to get free, but he held tight. He climbed into the boat with Malik, and the other man pushed them back into the water.

"You can have the dog back when you accept my offer," Malik said loudly. Malik and Nasir smiled smugly as the boat slid into the water. The engine roared, and they were gone.

Clyde spit blood and collapsed onto his face in the sand. It was dusk when he opened his eyes.

"Should have killed me," he said to himself.

He rolled onto his back and sat in the sand. He felt his damaged face gently. Everything was swollen. His shirt front was covered in mud and blood. He attempted to stand and go to the cabin. A sharp pain in his chest stopped him from moving. Clyde discovered he could crawl with limited pain, but it was slow going. He made it to the chair and sat for a long time. Finally, he staggered to his feet and struggled his way back to the cabin.

Once inside, he quickly grabbed his pistol and collapsed into his chair near the fire. The pistol remained in his lap with nothing but embers from the night before in the fire. Clyde drifted out of consciousness again. Time was lost to him. He awoke to darkness. He put his hand down to his side. Betsy was not there. It hadn't been a bad dream then.

With a resolute will, Clyde stood and made his way to the water. He was so thirsty. It hurt to drink. It hurt to breath. It hurt to do anything. He thought of nothing but survival. Survival, so he could inflict retribution on them that had done this to him.

"Betsy," he whispered. "I'm gonna make them pay."

CHAPTER 10

SECRETS

Ham saddled Sundance. His head was feeling better, if better meant it still throbbed, ached, and if he touched the wound the pain was staggering. Changing the bandage was an ugly affair. The wound itself was still raw and sensitive. The deepest part of the wound was seeping a clear fluid. Even so, the fogginess seemed to be going away. He was glad for it, as he knew he would need a clear head to tackle what lie ahead.

Ham settled into the saddle as Stripey appeared from the trees and stepped close to Sundance. Ham pulled a sugar cube from his pocket and tossed it to the ground in front of Stripey.

"Here you go. Hate to have you feel left out little guy," Ham said. "Sundance, I think you better adopt Stripey, he's definitely adopted you."

Ham listened to the sounds around him. All seemed as it should: a gentle breeze, a distant sound of water gurgling over rock, and an occasional bird. He clenched his thighs and Sundance walked off down the trail. Ham knew the way by now and felt at home on the trail toward the cabin. Magpies by the score took to flight as he passed the hog seep. Ham turned Sundance off the trail to have a closer look and noticed several hog carcasses with no heads.

Ham chuckled and shook his head, "What are you up to Clyde?"

Ham didn't dismount and kept on. No one came to greet him as he rode into the yard near the cabin. He didn't think it strange. Clyde could be anywhere. Ham slid the saddle and bridle off of Sundance and turned him loose. Ham's stomach growled as he reached the door. The growling disappeared as he noticed blood on the knob. He drew his pistol, and held his breath, listening...nothing.

He slowly turned the knob, and in one fluid motion he kicked the door open, stepping in. His eyes cleared the corners. Nothing but Clyde sitting in the chair by the fire, his pistol in his hand.

"What the hell happened to your head?" Clyde asked.

"What the hell happened to your face?" Ham asked.

"I was born too pretty, the devil's been trying to ruin it ever since. I was told you were dead."

"The rumors of my death have been greatly exaggerated," Ham said with a laugh.

"Glad for that. Guess they killed the zebras?" Clyde asked.

"I found them, but they were dead. I brought back one little baby zebra orphan though."

"A baby one?"

"Yep."

"Should just knock it in the head."

"I'm calling him Stripey," Ham added.

"How original."

"You're making fun of my name, when you named a striped Zorse, *Spot*?"

116

"Good point. So, what happened?"

"I caught them, cutting up the zebras. I was moving in for a look and someone shot me. A few centimeters, and I'd be laying out there, dead."

"Well, they think they killed you."

"I think I had a concussion. The wound is bad."

"They paid me a visit. Beat my ass and took Betsy hostage, the sonsabitches!" Clyde swore bitterly and stared into the flames burning as brightly as his rage.

"You alright?"

"Not really, but I'll live. I think they cracked a rib."

"What did they want?"

"They gave me three days to decide to sell this place to them."

"Fuck that," Ham said.

Clyde laughed. "Exactly what I told them. They took Betsy. I'm gonna kill them bastards if they hurt her. Actually, I'm gonna kill them fuckers either way."

Ham noticed a bottle of whiskey sitting on the table. He took a swig and sat down next to Clyde handing the bottle to him. He tipped it up and enjoyed a hearty swallow.

"Well, how we gonna do it?"

Clyde gave Ham a sideways glance and a slight smile.

"Tomorrow I have to show you something," Clyde said.

"What is it?"

"The heart of the ranch."

"The heart?"

"And all the secrets."

Ham just nodded as Clyde returned his stare to the fire.

"I'm starving. I'm going to cook something," Ham said.

"I have pork ribs over there. Let's grill 'em over a fire."

"Sounds good. I noticed you killed some bacon."

Clyde groaned as he stood from sitting. "Been sitting too long. Yeah, I didn't get 'em all, but I got a few of them. Then I took their heads and feet and put 'em all along the trail the A-rabs been sneaking around on. They hate all things pig. Thought it might scare 'em off for a while. I also rolled one of their four-wheelers into a ravine."

"Nice," Ham said as he grabbed the meat and followed Clyde out front. In short order a roaring fire licked at the ribs as they hung on the spit. Ham and Clyde sat staring at the fire. The meat sizzled, filling the air with a tantalizing aroma. Dusk turned to darkness, and the meat smoked to perfection. They ate in silence. Each alone with his thoughts as they shared a fine meal and the company.

Ham leaned back in his chair completely satisfied. "That was some fine swine."

"It's best over an open fire," Clyde agreed.

"You should let me butterfly that cut over your eye. I could close it up a bit and help it heal."

"I've been cut worse."

"Who did it?"

"It was Nasir and the new guy you fought with."

"Leroy?"

"Yeah, Malik was there too, but he didn't fight, just gave the order. They're gonna wish they'd killed me, taking my dog like this…"

"I had a dog as a kid," Ham said.

"Yeah? What kind?"

"Black Lab."

"They're a good dog."

"It got ran over while I was at school. Came home on the bus and it was laying there by the road. I started crying, everyone laughed at me. Called me cry-baby."

"Fuck those assholes," Clyde said with a vicious edge to his voice. He was obviously over the edge in a perpetual state of rage, like smoldering coals.

"I never cried again," Ham said.

Silence grew between them. Clyde continued his seething stare at the flames.

"That was a long time ago," Ham finally broke the silence.

"Well, sometimes a dog is all you got. A good dog can be a better friend than a lot of people."

"Yeah. We'll get Betsy back."

"Maybe," Clyde said. He slapped his knees and grunted as he stood up. "I gotta get some shut eye. I'll need it tomorrow with what I got planned." He ambled into the cabin.

"See you in the morning," Ham said. Clyde didn't answer.

The fire was down to embers, and a sea of stars blanketed the heavens above. As Ham stared up at The Big Dipper and The North Star, he smiled as it felt good to be under the North American night sky. He never got used to the different look to the stars in the Middle East.

"Wish you were here Mac. Trouble's following me everywhere I go," he whispered to himself. He wondered what Julie was doing right then. "She's probably already forgotten about me. On to the next cowboy..." *If I survive what's coming I'm gonna call her.* Ham found his room and was asleep almost the instant he lay flat.

First light found the two friends loading gear into their packs. Big Jake and Sundance stood saddled and ready in the yard. Stripey stood tightly next to Sundance's rear leg. Clyde filled Spot's trolley with several bags full of whatever he thought was needed. Ham finished loading all his gear and noticed Clyde still loading.

"Anything else?"

"Grab that last duffel, and we can go." Clyde pointed to a small bag laying by the door. Ham placed it in the cart.

"You look like you feel better today," Ham said.

"I'll survive. The damn rib hurts the most. How's your head?"

"Getting better. It's stopped leaking and only hurts when I touch it."

"Don't touch it then." Clyde climbed aboard Big Jake and turned him down the trail without another word.

Ham quickly gave Sundance and Stripey each a cube of sugar and mounted up. He trotted Sundance a short distance and settled in behind Big Jake. "So, where we goin'?"

"You'll see."

"I guess I'm on a need-to-know basis," Ham mumbled to himself. Sundance flicked an ear back in response.

Ham noticed they were on the far side of the valley walking along the steep side of the bluff. The valley wall was steep, but not a sheer cliff. An agile human could climb it, but it wouldn't be easy and some places were downright impassable. They began a slight incline as Ham noticed the green meadow that contained the hog seep below them in the distance.

The trail was thin and almost unnoticeable. Clyde suddenly turned hard left as if he would ride Big Jake right into the brush. A slight crease in the scrubby pines let them pass, but not without the prickly needles scraping both sides of horse and man. Ham raised his arm to protect his head. Even so, a branch slid along his wound. Shooting pain stabbed his head. "Damn," he said.

Stripey slid under the Pines easily keeping close to Sundance. Clyde dismounted and violently ripped some brush away from the path. Ham started to dismount to help.

"No, stay there." Clyde stepped out of the way and pointed to the opening he had cleared. "Lead the horses through, I gotta put the brush back."

Ham tightened his thighs on Sundance, and they entered what looked like a cave just wide enough for a man sitting on a horse in single file. Ham had little choice but to proceed. As the cave darkened around Ham he looked back over his shoulder to see Clyde back on Big Jake following along. The cave was obviously manmade. The ceiling was flat and squared off unlike a natural cave. Ham followed the cave which angled slightly downward until the brightness of the exit appeared just ahead. He blinked quickly as Sundance stepped into the light.

A small valley lay before him shaped almost perfectly round. Hardwoods mingled in a green pasture, and a small pool of water emptied into a creek along the far side. A slight smile came across Ham's face as he thought this might be his vision of Heaven.

"Nice huh?" Clyde said as he rode past Ham and continued down the narrow trail toward the valley floor.

"I guess. What other surprises you got for me?"

Clyde was too far ahead to answer. They sat their horses and let them take a deep drink from the clear pool. Trout could be seen in the crisp water.

"How much further?" Ham asked.

"None, we're there. C'mon." Clyde reined Big Jake into the largest stand of trees. The valley wasn't perfectly round. It was shaped more like a bean which shielded a small section from view from the entry point at the tunnel. Suddenly, a huge boulder field littered the side of the slope and at the apex a rectangular opening stood dark and ominous, both inviting and terrifying.

"A mine?" Ham asked.

"Yep. Ox bought this place when they shut it down, and it didn't pan out for them."

"What were they mining?"

"Gold."

"Really, a gold mine? They didn't find any?"

"They found all the signs of it, but never found the main vein and finally gave up."

"Like gambling nowadays…most never hit it big, but it's always out there, and no one ever finds it," Ham said.

"Oh, I wouldn't say *no one*," Clyde smiled as he dismounted.

"What do you mean?"

Clyde began taking off Big Jake's saddle. He noticed Ham just watching. "C'mon, get his stuff off. I got a lot to show you today."

Ham dismounted and quickly stripped Sundance's gear. Spot had followed them up the slope trail as they stood before the dark entrance to the mine. Clyde motioned for Ham to help as he unhitched Spot's cart. He let the tongue hit the ground and waved his arms at the horses. Effectively, pushing them back down the trail toward the green plateau below.

Clyde grabbed the cart. "C'mon, help me pull this inside."

Ham grasped the tongue of the cart and easily pulled it into the dark entrance of the mine.

Once inside, Clyde let go of the cart and pulled a head lamp from his pack. He handed one to Ham and put one on his own head turning it on. Ham put his lamp on over his hat, keeping the elastic from rubbing his wound. It felt better, but it wasn't healed. Ham turned his light on and followed along.

They travelled only about thirty yards, and they came to a metal door set in a wall of thick timbers. Above the door was a sign that read. *Hidden Valley Mine.* Then in smaller letters on the door it read. *Authorized Personnel Only.*

Clyde pulled a key from his pocket. "We're authorized."

He put the key in the latch and jiggled it just so as he turned it. He slammed his shoulder into the door, and it gave way opening inward. "She sticks a bit," Clyde said as he pushed it open and began unloading the cart. He set the bags just inside the open door. Ham helped without question. In a moment, the cart sat empty. Ham followed Clyde through the door. Clyde pushed hard against it, the metal creaking as it slammed closed behind them with the awful sound of a sealed tomb.

Clyde walked off into the darkness with his headlamp lighting the way. The air smelled dank, and the temperature was cool. They entered a room that appeared to be full of all kinds of tools. Clyde went to a large machine and squatted near the side of it. He reached under it and then stood.

"Gotta turn the gas on or she won't run," he said.

He turned a switch and instantly fired it up. The noise of the engine was deafening in the close quarters and blue smoke filled the air. Clyde pulled a cord near the outer wall and suddenly the smoke began lifting into a large dark opening in the stone overhead. Clyde smiled. He slammed his hand against a round button on the wall. Instantly, lights illuminated the entire tunnel leading off farther than Ham could see. The noise was still too loud to communicate easily. Clyde grabbed a couple duffels and began down the tunnel. Ham did likewise. They walked nearly fifty yards and came to another door. This one looked like an average wooden house door. Clyde entered it easily as it wasn't locked.

Ham followed. After Ham was in, Clyde shut the door behind them. Suddenly, the sound of the diesel engine was a distant hum. Clyde raised both hands to show the room.

"Welcome to what I call the *Foreman's Home.*"

Ham noticed an efficiency style apartment, complete with a couch, library of books, two beds, a wood burning stove, several wooden kegs, stores of food on shelves, a wash sink, a kitchen table complete with four chairs, and a framed picture of a chestnut horse hanging on the wall as artwork.

Clyde saw Ham admiring it, "Lloyd gave me that, long time ago. It's Man o' War, the racehorse."

"And people think the man cave is a new idea," Ham chuckled.

Clyde motioned to the kitchen table. "Grab a seat. Times a wastin'. I had planned to show you this if you earned the right. And to leisurely enjoy it with you as I have all these years, but events have accelerated beyond my control. Time is short."

Ham took a seat. Clyde spread a map on the table before him. "This is a map of the mine. It basically consists of a main lateral shaft and four horizontal shafts all running from the lateral. The lateral shaft has a functioning elevator. It runs on the diesel power, but if for whatever reason the diesel isn't running, it has a manual override to raise and lower it, but it's tough work, to do it manually. I will show you. I also have climbing pins and a ladder hooked to the wall of the shaft so you could climb out if the elevator is somehow not available or broken. You won't die at the bottom."

Ham looked at Clyde incredulously, "Does Lloyd know about this?"

"Yes, of course, he's my friend. He's the only one I've shown until now though. Anyway, I use the Foreman's Home as a retreat. It's always the same temperature… around fifty-five degrees. In the winter when it's negative ten outside it feels like the mine is heated. In the summer when it's ninety-five degrees it feels like we got central air. Really it's the earth's own geothermal."

"Is there gold?" Ham asked. His face incredulous.

"That's what everyone wonders? Follow me. I have to give you a full tour, double-time. Let's go."

Clyde grabbed the map and headed back through the door they came in. The apartment appeared to have no other entrance. They entered the elevator and Clyde handed the map to Ham. "Here you go. Memorize it." Clyde slammed an overhead cage down and latched it tight. He hit a faded green button with an arrow pointing downward. Instantly, the elevator creaked and groaned and began descending. It only went down about thirty feet when Clyde stopped the descent by hitting a red button that read, Stop.

Clyde slid the gate upward and stepped off the elevator. He hit a button on the side wall and lights illuminated along the ceiling into the distance disappearing around the curve of a horizontal mine shaft. "If you notice the tracks. Each shaft has a rail cart that was used to bring material out of the shaft back to the elevator. This shaft is nothing special. It goes about 300 yards and stops. A bunch of abandoned junk at the end. Let's keep on to the next one."

Clyde turned the lights off, climbed into the elevator, and slammed the gate shut. They began to descend further. They dropped deeper into the earth. Ham was glad for his jacket as it was cool and damp. Clyde halted the elevator. He shone his light into the cavern. "Nothing special about the second shaft either, except you should know that I've hidden food, water, ammo, a first aid kit, and essentials in the furthermost point of each horizontal boring. It is hidden in between the tracks at the very end of them. There is a stash box buried there right between the tracks. Also, these two shafts have two connecting shafts no bigger than two or three feet wide running between them, connecting one to the other. It was designed to let air pass, but if you can climb, they are not on the map…and allow secretive passage between the main shafts. One is about half way in; the other at the end of shaft two."

"That could come in handy," Ham said with a smile.

"Yes, it could."

They descended to the third shaft and exited the elevator. "Let's go have a look," Clyde said.

"Okay, what's up with this shaft?"

"It's by far the longest. It goes more than a mile. It also contains a makeshift mess area and a barracks of sorts with bunks for twenty men. C'mon, I'll show you if you're quick about it."

Ham followed Clyde as he quickly shuffled along the path lined with two metal tracks.

"There you go."

Ham could see a series of bunk bed style racks. "Could you sleep there?" Clyde asked.

"I've slept in worse."

Clyde smiled, "Exactly why you're the guy."

"I'm the guy for what?"

"They found a small trace line of gold in this shaft. That's why it's the biggest. They thought they'd hit the mother lode with this one. Never turned out enough to amount to much, and eventually they gave up and sold the mine. Anyway, no need to show you the bottom. Just a small shaft there. Lots of debris. No rails. The kind of place that if you hid there, better be ready to die there. No way out at the bottom of a deep hole." They climbed back in the elevator, and Clyde slammed the cage shut. Ham looked down. He couldn't see anything but darkness.

"Here's where it gets interesting," Clyde said with a wry smile.

CHAPTER 11

GOLD

Clyde turned a lever to *Up*, and then hit the green button. The metal cage began ascending amidst moans and creaks that would make most people wonder if crashing to the bottom might happen at any moment. Ham noticed Clyde staring at the rock wall as it slipped past. He was looking for something on the opposite side of the vertical shaft than where the horizontal mine shafts had been.

"What you looking for?" Ham hollered above the noise of the cage.

Clyde quickly hit the red stop button bringing the cage to a swinging halt seemingly between shafts two and three.

Clyde handed a backpack to Ham, "You're stronger than me."

"Yeah, but I recently got shot in the head."

"It bounced off, you're fine. You want me to carry it?"

"No, I was just kidding," Ham said as he settled the straps onto his shoulders. Both men had their headlamps on and were dressed warmly for the coolness of the earth's depths.

Clyde pointed to a metal ladder on the opposing wall. "See the ladder?"

"Yeah," Ham answered.

"It goes all the way to the bottom, like I said, but some of it is just spikes. I was working on it one day. It was years ago now, and found this. C'mon. This ain't on the map either."

Clyde climbed out of the cage and onto the metal ladder. He disappeared downward. Ham took a deep breath and followed. The cold metal from the ladder was moist and rusted. Ham noticed Clyde's light completely disappear below him.

"Clyde? Where are you?" Ham shouted. He hadn't fallen or Ham would have seen. He descended a few more feet to find a ragged hole no bigger than a couple feet wide, it was a crack in the side wall. He could see light inside promising Clyde was already in. Ham's backpack rubbed on the stone as he pulled himself inside. He was forced to crawl a few feet as the crack opened into a cavern. Clyde stood in the center of the room with a huge grin on his face.

"What do you think?" he asked.

"Nice, if you're Batman. What's this?"

"This is what the miners were looking for and never found. I was working on the ladder and felt a slight wind coming through a crack in the rock wall. I gave it the slightest tap, and boom, she fell open, and I found this place. They missed it by inches."

"A cave?"

"Not just any cave. The mother lode. Look over here." Clyde pointed to a side wall only to have it glitter and sparkle in the light. "Gold and lots of it."

Ham's mouth sort of dropped open in awe.

"I just hack out a few chunks a year. It pays the taxes on the ranch and buys supplies. I give some to Lloyd for all his help."

"You never wanted to mine it? It could be worth millions," Ham asked.

"It is worth millions, but what's that to me? I just want to be left alone on my ranch. If people or the government knew this was here…they'd be mining the hell out of the whole region. Nope, I just take what I need, like a crop," Clyde said as he picked up a couple golf ball sized nuggets in his open palm, handing one to Ham.

Ham stared at it intently. "Never seen anything like this before."

"You probably never will again either. This is a special place."

"That's for sure," Ham agreed.

"Well there's more to this cavern than gold," Clyde said.

"What else?"

Clyde pointed to an opening off to the side of the massive cavern. "It goes for miles. I've mapped a fair amount of it."

"Where does it go?"

"I don't know, I never found the end, but it does go one place I've found, and we're going there now. C'mon let's go," Clyde walked toward the opening.

"Go? Go where?"

"This cave intersects the old mine over at Lone Wolf Canyon."

"No shit," Ham was incredulous.

"No shit, c'mon. It's a few miles and follow me closely. There are some places in here where a fall might not be a good idea."

"Okay, why are we going there?"

"Recon. I want Betsy back."

"All I have is a sidearm, we aren't ready to go to war with those guys you know?" Ham answered.

"I know. Their day is coming, but I needed to show you all this stuff, just in case, well, you know. Anyway, if I can grab Betsy or find out what they did with her, that's all I want today. Agreed?"

"Agreed."

Clyde continued down a makeshift trail. Ham noticed occasional tracks from a raccoon or opossum, but other than that the cave was bound in darkness. Their every movement echoed in the deathly silence. The cavern was large enough to walk easily upright and each turn brought on a stunning view of stone architecture. Clyde walked in silence.

"Wow," Ham exclaimed at a particularly breathtaking scene. "You've mapped this?"

Clyde paused to answer, "Yeah, but I only have a couple copies. It's not on any of the mining maps so no one knows it's here, but Lloyd and me, and now you."

"It's amazing in here," Ham said in awe.

"Yeah it is. Another half hour, and we'll be there."

Clyde turned his lamp to the darkness and continued on. Ham smiled as he watched the old man walk off for a moment before following. The cave seemed to suddenly descend sharply. They were forced to climb over boulders and even skid down a few. Ham wondered how easy getting back out would be for Clyde.

They reached an oblong-shaped room. Ham could see animal tracks leading into a small pool of dark water still as glass.

"What's this?" Ham asked.

"You'll see. You can swim, right?"

Ham laughed, "Yeah, I swim like a fish."

"Good." Clyde turned Ham around and began digging through the backpack. He pulled out a couple chem-lights blazing like a green sun.

"Glow sticks, nice," Ham said.

Clyde turned off his headlamp. "Turn yours off."

Ham did as commanded. It took a moment for their eyes to adjust to the glowing green sticks of illumination.

"Leave the backpack here. We will get it on the way back," Clyde said. He laid his headlamp on top of it and turned to the pool. He opened the action on his pistol to be sure a round was chambered. "When I found this place, I was sitting here having a piece of jerky thinking about the climb back up the rocks when a son-of-a-bitchin' muskrat popped his head up in the pool. Scared the hell out of me and him. He disappeared back under the water. I figured it must go somewhere. The first time I tried it, my flashlight died in the water about half way through. That was fuckin' fun!"

"I bet." Ham un-holstered his weapon and made sure his extra mags were in their loops on his belt. He held the pistol in his hand.

"Anyway, it's cold, but it's clear. You can open your eyes and see with these lights. There is a boulder submerged about two feet that runs for a good ten to fifteen feet. If you try to come up to soon, you'll hit your head. The pool on the other side doesn't have any beach area like this. It's a solid rock wall at the bottom of a thirty-foot hole. You have to dog paddle around until you find the ledge. There is a way to go up the rock, but it's tricky. Just follow me the first time. You'll be fine. If I can do it, it'll be cake for you."

Ham nodded. His adrenaline was pumping. It felt good to be on a mission. It felt so good, he almost felt guilty.

"What's with the guns?" Ham asked.

"Well, last I knew they've not figured out the pool goes anywhere, and they don't use the cave for anything. The mine part is near the surface and is just full of junk, but you never know. Hate to come out of the water and find some camel jockey waiting for us there. There wouldn't be any time to draw. We'd be fish in a barrel. Literally. With the guns, we could return fire and grab a breath and swim back under. Understood."

"Understood?"

"Let's go," Clyde said. He was all business as he waded into the pool up to his knees. The rock underfoot was slippery.

Clyde smiled at Ham and took a deep breath. With a light stick in one hand, and his pistol in the other he dove forward headfirst into the dark water. Ham watched as his glow stick disappeared under the rock. Ham inhaled deeply and followed Clyde.

The water was cold. Ham's senses were alive as he swam strongly toward the glow light ahead. He burst through the surface on the other side with a quiet precision that belied his discipline. No sound of water splashing or a loud exhale. Ham was just suddenly there. Clyde was already pulling himself up the sheer of the rock walls encircling the pool.

"Nobody here. Just us. The only way out is over here. Follow me," Clyde said.

Ham followed Clyde up the stone. Slight clefts in the rock made for climbing holds. Ham was rather surprised at the toughness of the old man. At times, he seemed like he could hardly walk across the room and here he was scaling a rock wall in a cave of absolute darkness. His admiration and fondness for Clyde was growing. Clyde felt like the father that he should have had.

They made it to the top and squatted on a round boulder. Clyde was breathing heavily. "Let me catch my damn breath. It's no more than couple hundred yards to the surface. So be quiet, but there's probably nobody around. They do most of their training down on the valley floor near the cabins from what I've seen."

"How much have you seen?" Ham said with a whisper.

"I've watched them a few times, to see what they were up to. I've seen them doing some conditioning, some crawling, and some basic training. Marksmanship at targets. They're not very good. That's about it. Okay, I'm good, let's go." Clyde stood and headed off into the darkness, his pistol still in his hand.

There was a trail of sorts, but much of it was just rock boulders to climb over, and it made for slow going. Clyde suddenly dropped the glow stick into his pocket and pressed himself against a boulder. Ham did likewise. Darkness settled over them. Ham could see light up ahead. They crept slowly toward it. They entered what was obviously a section of the mine. Round ceilings and flat floors, definitely man made. As they inched forward, a room came into view. A lamp was on sitting upon a desk littered with papers. Metal kegs of beer filled the cavern.

Ham leaned close to Clyde and whispered, "Beer kegs?"

"None of this used to be here. It used to be full of junk."

Ham scanned the room and noticed copper wire, electronics, cell phones in pieces, and what looked to be several shelves lined with explosives.

"Making bombs," Ham whispered.

"Yep, motherfuckers," Clyde swore viciously. "No one's here. I want to look out and see if I can locate Betsy."

Clyde marched right through the bomb lab and out the open door letting the light stream in. Ham followed, but stopped in his tracks at the desk. His stomach sank.

Blueprints titled AT&T Stadium caught his attention. A big star in the corner.

"What the fuck, Cowboy Stadium?" Ham said as he sifted through the papers. He immediately noticed that each concession stand in the stadium was marked with yellow highlighter. Notes about each entrance into the stadium were written in red ink. The delivery locations and keg storage areas were all marked as well.

Ham suddenly looked over the field of silver beer kegs. He noticed several of them had been cut open from the bottom. A false bottom had been installed that would allow a few gallons of beer to still be in the top portion and make the keg function normally. The bottom section was entirely rigged and packed full of explosives and wire accompanied by an electronic trigger mechanism.

Ham quickly grabbed the set of blueprints and folded them up sticking them in the back of his pants and under his shirt. He stepped up behind Clyde who was crouching and staring out into the bright sunlight. A beautiful green valley much like theirs presented itself below.

"Look," Clyde pointed. "There she is tied to the flag pole." A black flag with white Arabic lettering gently flittered in the wind. Betsy lay on the ground panting in the sun.

Just then a couple of men walked past Betsy. The man closest to her kicked her viciously and without warning. She rolled with an audible whimper. Clyde lunged forward. "Son-of-a…" He clenched his teeth as Ham grabbed his shoulder from behind to keep him from charging down the hill.

Clyde shook Ham's hand off of his shoulder, blind with rage. Suddenly, two men entered the white light of the mine shaft marching straight toward them. Clyde instinctively crouched behind a stack of boxes, while Ham pressed himself tight to the sidewall. The men were blind from the outside light and walked right past them into the bomb lab.

Clyde looked at Ham and shrugged. Ham just shook his head in return. Bad luck. Sometimes when you're holding eights, you draw aces. The two men were now solidly between Clyde and Ham, absolutely blocking their escape at the back of the cave. Ham knew what had to be done. He gave Clyde a smile and a wink as he walked into the bomb lab.

"Hiya fellas. Making some keg bombs are we?" Both men jumped at his words, terror crossing their faces. The man closest to Ham lunged at him. Ham swung a hard left and caught the man square in the nose sending him to his knees, blood streaming down his face. The man cried out and put his hands to his nose only to see them covered with blood.

Clyde stood off to Ham's left covering the man who stood by the desk with his sidearm. Ham motioned for the bloody nosed fellow to stand up with the gun he held in his right hand. The man did not obey, but kept carrying on about his broken nose.

"You don't want to fire those guns in here," the man near the desk spoke fine English with only a hint of accent. "You see, if this stuff goes off, this whole cave will come down on us."

"Shut the fuck up," Clyde said. "Can I shoot him?"

"Maybe," Ham said. "He's right about the bombs. Can you hit him right in the middle?"

"Yeah," Clyde said as he aimed the weapon right at the man's chest causing his face to turn ashen white.

The bloody nosed man started speaking in Arabic. Ham knew bits and pieces of the language, but not enough to comprehend what he was saying. It sounded like a prayer as many times as he kept hearing the word, *Allah*.

"Shut the hell up," Ham demanded of the bloody nosed man.

The man acted as if he was deaf to Ham's demands. Ham stepped close and kicked the man in the leg. "I said shut up!"

While Ham's attention was focused on the bloody nosed man, the man near the desk quickly pulled a knife from under a stack of papers on the desk.

"Stop right there Sandman, or I'll shoot your ass and bring this mountain down," Clyde said. "I'm old, what do I care?"

The man smiled a bit and readied himself on the balls of his feet. He shifted the wide, curved knife from hand-to-hand as if he'd handled it all his life.

"What the fuck are you going to do with that?" Ham asked. "Against two guns?"

The man laughed, "This is a sacred Janbiya. It has been in my family for many generations. My father gave it to me, and I will gut you both with it."

Ham glanced at the sleek black weapon in his hand. "This is a Glock. My good friend Clyde gave it to me, and you better warm up that pecker you goat-humping-bastard cause it's gonna send you to meet a whole mess of virgins!"

Without warning the bloody nosed man seized his opportunity and bolted for the light screaming *Allahu Akbar, Allahu Akbar!*

Ham was forced to lunge after him. He grabbed the back of the man's shirt just as he was about to escape the mine. His shouts carried out into the valley. Ham couldn't be sure if anyone was near enough to hear his screams.

Ham threw him to the ground hard. The man coughed the air from his lungs as he swirled in a cloud of dust and came up with a knife of his own. He slashed laterally forcing Ham to jump back. Ham felt the bite of cold steal clip his forearm. The slash had left the man half turned and off balance. Ham's training was a part of him. Without any thought, he immediately stepped in close and grabbed hold of the man around his neck. Ham squeezed with all his strength.

The man would have screamed if he had any air. Ham's forearm and bicep were pinching his throat. Ham's face snarled as he gave the man's head a sharp twist. An awful crunching sound emanated from the bloody nose man as his neck snapped, and his body went immediately limp. Ham dropped his body and turned his attention toward Clyde.

He saw the man near the desk was on top of Clyde with his Janbiya pressing down toward Clyde, the tip of it already drawing blood on Clyde's chest. Clyde had both of his hands pressing up against the other man's hands straining with all his strength to keep the blade from plunging through his sternum. Clyde's face was turning red as he grimaced against the strength of the younger man. It was obvious he was about to give way.

Ham sprinted to them. It was only a few steps. He placed his pistol against the ribs of the Clyde's attacker just under the armpit and fired a single round through his rib cage spraying blood and bits of heart and lungs all over the wall with the exit wound. The shot rang through the mine and echoed to the depths as the man slumped over and dropped his knife onto Clyde's chest.

Nothing exploded, and the cave didn't collapse. Much of the noise from the shot had been absorbed by the dead man's body, but not all of it. "If they didn't hear that fucking guy screaming *Aloha Snack bar*, they definitely heard that shit. "Let's go! Can you walk?" Ham asked.

Clyde pulled himself from under the dead man and stood. He was covered in blood.

"You alright?" Ham asked.

"Yeah, the blood's mostly his."

Raised voices could be heard from just outside the mine. Obviously, the sound of the shot had not gone unnoticed. Clyde glanced around to get his bearings and then led off back down into the cave the way they had come.

CHAPTER 12

They skidded and slid as they ran as fast as the rocky trail would permit. Suddenly, they stood on the precipice with nothing but darkness below. Clyde glanced at Ham, "This is gonna be fun. Try to jump straight in. Off to the side is rocks and all kinds of stuff that will hurt. So, jump straight in...and then swim through, just like before."

A bright light and Arabic shouting was getting closer from behind. "No problem," Ham said. "Jump straight."

"See ya on the other side," Clyde said as he took two big steps and dropped into the darkness. Ham heard the splash and watched as his glow light disappeared. The voices behind were getting louder. He took two steps and held his breath as he fell. The cold water attacked his senses. Clyde's light was a beacon, and he swam for it. He burst forth from the water with a splash and a big breath.

Clyde grabbed his arm, and they climbed out of the water together. Clyde immediately sat next to the backpack they had left behind. He stuffed his glow light inside it and rested his arms on his knees pointing his pistol at the water, ready for anything that might follow them through. "Put your light in the bag, they might be able to see it. And get ready in case any of these guys are brave enough to try it."

Ham slammed his light into the bag. Darkness fell upon them. Real darkness. The kind that no matter how long your eyes tried, they don't ever adjust. Cave darkness.

Ham listened for sounds and waited for anyone following them through the water. For a time, they could hear muffled sounds from the other side, but they dissipated until absolute silence joined the darkness. The only sounds were from them breathing.

Ham could hear Clyde stirring. Suddenly, a blinding light exploded through the black night like a stream of daylight. Clyde fixed his headlamp onto his head and handed one to Ham. "You didn't have to shoot him."

"What?" Ham questioned.

"I had it under control," Clyde said with a look of thanks on his face.

"I know you did. I just thought we should hurry," Ham said as he patted the older man's shoulder.

"We better get going. I need to go to the cabin. After this, they'll hit it, and there are a few things I need."

"We shouldn't go back to the cabin," Ham answered.

"I didn't bring everything we need. We'll have time to beat them there and back to the mine. They'll take some time to think before they come after us. In the mine, they can't take us," Clyde said confidently.

Ham didn't like it. He knew it was a bad idea to go back to the cabin. It was utterly indefensible and sat near the easiest method of transportation, the river. With their fast boats, they could easily be at the cabin before he and Clyde made it back there.

Clyde marched like a man on a mission. His age appeared all over his face as he looked ragged and old. However, he marched as if he was twenty years old and strong. They were covering ground quickly and only stopped occasionally for a drink and a quick bite of jerky from the pack. The journey back seemed to be much shorter than the trail to the pool. Everything moves faster when it feels like the clock is ticking. The gold room appeared just up ahead. The sparkling rock was ablaze in the light of the headlamps.

Malik strode slowly into the bomb lab, Nasir on his flank. Malik stepped over the body of the bloody nosed man as if it was a sack of Idaho spuds. He squatted near the body of the other man peering at his face frozen in death.

"Nasir?"

"Yes."

"How many kegs are ready?"

"More than one hundred, I think."

"That is enough for the mission. We must begin transport to the warehouse in Texas."

"Yes, right away."

"Not right away," Malik said as he picked up the Janbiya laying in a pool of blood. He held it up watching light dance on the blade as the blood ran down his arm. "First, we must kill these men. The blood of my brother cries out for vengeance."

"These?" Nasir asked.

"Surely you don't think one old man did this, do you?"

Nasir tried not to look surprised, "But we killed the other one."

"I think not," Malik said. "Send a team to the ridge to watch the cabin from above. Let me know if they are there. Do not let them know of your presence and do not attack. No four-wheelers, understood?"

"Yes. It will be done." Nasir began backing away from Malik, his head slightly bowed.

"And bring me the dog," Malik said with a sick smile on his face.

"The dog?" Nasir asked.

"Yes, and don't hurt it. Just bring it to me."

They hurried out of the mine and gathered the horses. They both went about their work with almost no conversation. Clyde led the way on Big Jake with Ham following along on Sundance as was their habit. They had kept the other animals secured in the hidden valley, but nothing could keep Stripey from following Sundance.

The little zebra never left his side. Sundance didn't seem to mind. Clyde cantered the majority of the way back to the cabin. Both horses were lathered and tiring, but Clyde pressed on. Clyde stopped and dismounted a few hundred yards from the cabin. The horses were glad for the rest. They grazed lush meadow grass as Clyde and Ham crept forward for a look.

The cabin appeared deserted, just like it should be. They watched for an hour with no sign of anything.

"Is there any way to contact Lloyd?" Ham asked.

"No."

"When do you think he'll be back?"

"Hard to say. He usually comes twice a month, but he keeps his own schedule," Clyde said with a gruff snap to his voice.

"You know we need to get out of here, right?" Ham asked.

"I ain't going nowhere. Those assholes can git, if anyone goes."

"I know, but there's too many of them for the two of us to take, and we need to tell the FBI or somebody about the keg bombs. This is bigger than just us."

"You can go. I ain't going nowhere." Clyde stared at his cabin. "I don't think anyone is around. Let's go down. Won't take but a few minutes to grab my stuff, and we can head back to the mine."

"Okay. How hard would it be to ride out of here?" Ham asked.

"There's a partial trail through a couple million acres. Take you a few days if you don't get lost."

"How about one of the rafters floating by?"

"Some of them could give you a lift or some of them have Sat phones, but I ain't going." Clyde groaned as he clambered to his feet and strode off toward the cabin.

Ham had no choice but to follow along. Clyde carried his pistol in his right hand swinging at his side. Ham held his lever gun deftly in both hands as he walked. His eyes scanned the edges of surrounding hillside piercing through the brush in search of anything that was human. He was uneasy as the surrounding ridges provided plenty of cover for watching eyes and were within shot range from several vantage points. Ham didn't like that Clyde was walking so boldly in the open. He should be keeping to the trees more than he was, but there was no reasoning with him now. His anger had taken hold and only one thing was going to abate it. Blood.

Clyde sauntered right into the cabin and began gathering his things. Ham didn't have anything inside so he stood guard from a small stand of trees near the corner of the cabin. He had a good view of the front of the cabin most of the way to the river. After a few minutes, Clyde exited the cabin carrying a small leather pack slung over his shoulder. Ham could tell it was heavy by the way it affected Clyde's motion. He placed it at Ham's feet, the sound of metal clinking as it settled to the ground.

"I forgot one last thing," Clyde said as he turned back to the cabin.

"Well, get it all, because we aren't likely to be back soon."

The roar of a fast boat cruising up the river brought Clyde from the cabin. He stood in the door frame. The noise quieted for a moment, then escalated as the boat loudly sped away.

Ham saw her first. "Oh...fuck," he whispered and raised his rifle to his shoulder.

Betsy stumbled into Clyde's view and stopped thirty yards from the cabin. She whined and looked at Clyde with eyes pleading for help. Tears welled up in Clyde's old eyes at the sight of her. She had a back pack of sorts strapped to her. It hung on both sides and had a couple visible wires sticking from the top of it.

"Clyde?"

"Yeah," he answered without taking his eyes from Betsy.

"They got her wired good," Ham said.

"I can see it."

"There's probably somebody up on the ridge with a detonator watching till she gets close enough."

Clyde didn't answer. His pulse could be seen on a vein in his neck. His mind was racing. He was tempted to rush toward her and die with his friend.

"Betsy, good girl, you're a good girl..." he soothed.

She took a couple steps toward Clyde. She was quivering. You could tell she wanted to run to Clyde and lick his face and go sit in the chair like they had done a thousand times.

"Stay girl, stay," Clyde said. "What can we do?"

"I got her," Ham said.

"Son-of-a-bitch." Clyde wiped his eyes with the back of his hand. "Good girl Betsy. You're a good girl. Best dog I ever had. You're a good girl."

Betsy took another step toward them and stopped. She could sense something was terribly wrong.

"Ham?"

"Yeah."

"Can you promise me you'll hit her in the eye? I don't want her to feel nothing."

"I got her, Clyde, she won't feel it. I promise." Ham steadied his rifle against one of the trees. The open sight settled exactly on the black of her right eye. A tear slipped from Ham's eye.

"I'm gonna talk to her. You just do it when you know you won't miss."

"Okay, Clyde."

Betsy whined loudly.

"You're a good girl, Betsy. Good girl. I'll see you soon. Good girl. You're my good gi…"

Boom! The rifle bucked in Ham's arms. Betsy dropped like a rock. The bullet had entered her skull through the eye, just as Ham had promised. She was instantly dead.

Nasir stood on the ridge above with a clear view of the front of the cabin. He jumped at the sound of the shot. When he noticed that the dog was down, he swore bitterly in Arabic. He hadn't expected they'd put her down. He quickly hit *send* on the cell phone he held in his hand.

Instantly, the ordnance strapped to the dog exploded with a ferocious sound. Dust and shrapnel flew through the air. Nasir gathered his men and commanded them back to camp to report to Malik.

Ham and Clyde both hit the dirt at the explosion. Dust and searing hot metal filled the space around where Betsy had stood. Both men were safely outside the blast radius. Ham jumped to his feet and scanned the ridge. He glimpsed movement. The rifle instantly was on his shoulder and began barking its own retort. He was firing as fast as he could work the lever. He didn't have a good target; but he was confident, and angry enough to lay down some serious fire in the general direction of where he'd seen the motion.

Nasir's men hit the ground as hot lead whizzed overhead and crashed through the brush. They snuck away as they attempted to stay concealed. One man hit the ground with a thud. Nasir grabbed him by the shoulder and dragged him to his footing as they staggered away. His face was white, and bright red blood splashed the ground behind him. The bullet had entered through his shoulder blade and come out through his right upper chest. He was spitting up frothy, bright-colored blood, but he kept his feet, not wanting to get left behind. It wasn't long before he collapsed, gurgling his last breath. They piled brush over him and left him on the trail back to their camp. Malik was not going to be pleased. They'd lost another man and only killed a dog.

The trigger clicked in Ham's hands. He lowered the weapon and turned to find Clyde standing near the small crater in the dirt where Betsy had stood. Ham stepped up and stood shoulder-to-shoulder with him. The explosion hadn't left much behind. Clyde stooped and picked up a piece of gray fur. He unconsciously stroked it between his thumb and forefinger. Suddenly, Ham felt uneasy and realized they stood in the open. Easy targets.

"Let's go. We need to take cover and get to the mine," Ham said.

Clyde's lower lip quivered, and he looked old and tired.

"Clyde…let's go."

His eyes hardened on Ham into a stare that actually startled Ham.

"I'm gonna kill those fuckers," Clyde said.

"I know. We will. We gotta get to cover."

"We? I thought you were leaving."

"C'mon let's get to the mine. We'll make a plan."

CHAPTER 13

RETRIBUTION

Clyde exhaled deeply as he settled into a chair at the table in the Foreman's Home. Ham sat across from him. Ham tilted his head back drinking deeply from his canteen. He replaced the lid and hung it on the back of the chair. Clyde got up and retrieved a cask of dark beer and two glasses. He filled each cup and turned to the stove. He opened the front door and stirred the fire. Ham stood. "Let me do that."

Surprisingly Clyde didn't argue and sat down at the table as Ham began frying some salt pork and heating some water for a soup. It wasn't much, but it beat an MRE.

"You gonna be alright?" Ham asked.

"Yeah, I guess I loved that dumb dog more than I thought."

"She was a good one."

"The best."

Ham lifted his glass. "To Betsy, a good dog, and a good friend."

Clyde clinked his glass to Ham's and took a solid drink.

"What are you thinking about over there?" Ham asked as he placed a plate of food in front Clyde. Clyde took a bite and chewed silently for a moment.

"Well, they have to hit us. After what we did to the bomb guys, we know too much; we've seen too much. They must've hoped Betsy would've ran right to me and killed us both. Since that didn't work..."

"They'll have to kill us before we get out or expose them." Ham said. "They'll be watching the river."

"Yeah, and they'll be coming, but I doubt they've found this place. They'll hit the cabin."

"You realize we should hit the trail at first light. A few days ride, and we can be away from all this. Call the Feds. Send in the Cavalry. We can come back after they clean 'em out."

Clyde nodded silently. "Yeah, makes sense I guess. Or we could just hole up here for a few days. Lloyd will be coming any day now. I don't think I can make that ride out, even if I agreed to it, which I don't."

A look of doubt spread over Ham's face, "You could make that ride, if you wanted to. I've seen how tough you are."

Clyde shook his head side-to-side, "I'm more tired than tough. If you want to go, I can hole up here alone. They won't be able to get me out of here once I seal it up tight."

"I don't like the idea of leaving you behind."

"Don't worry about me. I've been alone out here for years. Worst case is I end up in the valley next to old Ox. That ain't so bad."

Ham just shook his head at the stubborn old man.

Clyde opened up the leather pack that he had gathered at the cabin.

"What was so important we had to go after?" Ham asked.

Clyde lay a hand grenade on the table next to the deck of cards.

"Oh, I see," Ham said. "Where'd you get those?"

Clyde continued unloading more grenades until eight of them lay between them. "Ol' Lloyd has connections. We used to blow beaver dams with them once in a while."

"What are you planning to do with them now?" Ham asked.

"Nothing. I just didn't want them to have them."

"Did you see all the explosive stuff they had?"

Clyde shrugged, "Yeah, well, these are mine. I didn't want them to fall into enemy hands." Clyde laid two envelopes on the table labeled in his scrawling hand. One read, *Ham*, the other *Lloyd*.

"These are all the important papers if I was to say, *accidentally*, fall down the mine shaft or get blown up by my dog. I'm giving them to you. Don't open them unless I'm gone. Understand?"

"Yeah, you shouldn't talk like this," Ham said.

"I want no regrets. Gotta make plans sometimes. You promise me you'll give Lloyd his?"

"I promise."

"He'll know what to do with it."

Ham lay the documents he stole from the bomb room on the table before them. He began examining them.

"They're gonna blow that whole dang stadium. That thing holds a hundred-thousand people if it's full. Those beer kegs will be spaced evenly all around the place. If they went off all at once?"

"A big fuckin' boom," Clyde said.

"Yeah, wouldn't kill everyone, probably, but it would outdo 9-11, and it's America's team and all that symbolism. These terrorist asses love that stuff."

"Well, they won't get a chance to do it. You're gonna tell the cops, and these guys are going away."

"Yeah. I guess."

"And then I can have my life back and live out my old age in peace," Clyde said.

"That cave is a perfect hiding place for these bomb makers. No satellites could see them, no drones, nothing, just a harmless summer camp. Right?" Ham asked.

"Yeah, harmless. Killed a harmless dog. Cowards."

"Oh, Betsy. Maybe you can get a new dog?"

"Nope. She was the last dog for me." Clyde refilled their glasses, and sat back in his chair. "If I was younger, I'd take these grenades and I'd sneak in close and blow those fuckers to pieces just before sunup. I know a secret trail down."

"Of course you do. You have all the secrets."

"I'd do it, don't think I wouldn't." Clyde said with a stern face.

"I don't doubt you, Clyde, but to take that camp, we'd need at least a good four-man team of my bros and all our gear. If you went in there alone, not much chance of success, young or old."

"Depends on what you call success," Clyde smiled.

"I guess."

Clyde emptied his glass. "Time for me to hit the rack."

"Me too," Ham agreed.

They each found their way to the bunks along the outer wall. Clyde was seemingly instantly asleep as a rhythmic snore was emanating from his bunk. Ham lay on his back in the darkness. Red coals glowing in the open door of the stove. His mind racing. He knew he should force Clyde to join him on the ride out. The stubborn old coot wouldn't listen. He saw Julie in his mind as he finally drifted to sleep.

Ham jumped awake. The room was completely dark as the coals had burned out. He quickly turned on his headlamp.

"Shit." Clyde was gone and so were the hand grenades. Ham quickly donned his outer shell and grabbed his pack. He carried his rifle as he exited the mine. He could see Sundance grazing below with Stripey right by his side, but there was no sign of Big Jake.

"That old son-of-a-bitch. I should have known." Ham swore as he hurried down the slope carrying his saddle over his shoulder. Sundance saw him coming and meandered his way looking for a sugar cube.

"Sorry boy, I don't have any today." He saddled up and headed out of the hidden valley. Once he was out and had replaced the brush, he climbed aboard Sundance.

"Where's he going?"

"I know where he's going, but how do I get there. Damn him and his secret trails." Ham fanned out in a half circle looking for sign. He noticed a half track and a scuffed rock heading right up the side of the rock face. Without any hesitation, he clicked his heels to Sundance, and he bounded up the steep section to discover a very steep but manageable game trail hidden amongst the trees and boulders. It wound its way ever higher. Jake's hoof prints were fresh. Ham ignored the fact that Stripey followed along. His only thoughts were Clyde. They reached the ridge line and followed the main trail for a long way. They exited the trees, and Ham found himself with a wide-open plateau before him. He pulled out his binoculars and scanned the distant tree line. He caught a flash of movement and white fur. Half a dozen bighorn sheep grazed the tall grass.

"Ah...there you are."

Ham could see Big Jake covering ground fast with Clyde riding hell bent for leather. They disappeared into the trees more than a mile away. Ham squeezed Sundance and they lit out toward where Ham had marked Clyde's disappearance into the wood. The plateau between the trees turned out to be deceptively *not* flat. Ham found himself on the edge of a steep precipice and no way to cross. It was like a tear had opened up in the ground no more than fifty feet across, but deep. He was forced to back track.

Ham reined Sundance around and turned north hoping to find a way around. "Dang it, Clyde."

A half hour later Ham found a way around and spurred Sundance on. He was lathered by the time they reached the tree line, and Ham had lost his mark. All the pines looked the same from close up. He walked the tree line hoping to cut sign. Every minute meant Clyde was further away.

Ham turned back on himself, sure he'd missed it. He took a deep breath and focused on his task. Searching the ground for any clue that Big Jake had gone through here. A smile came across Ham's face. He noticed a bush with a freshly broken twig. He turned Sundance and found the trail plain as day.

With no warning...the sound of an explosion echoed through the woods. Ham tensed. The sound was a distance off, but it was definitely a grenade. Ham spurred Sundance. He was a sure-footed animal, but he ran down the trail much faster than was safe, skidding and sliding more than once.

"Careful boy," Ham spoke soothingly while pushing him on just the same. Two more explosions followed in short succession.

"Damn it, Clyde," he whispered to himself. Ham glimpsed the valley through the trees as it dropped off below. There was a trail along the ridge well-worn with four-wheeler tracks. Ham suddenly realized he better beware of sentries. He held his breath listening as he scanned the area. He heard nothing but screaming down below in Arabic. Black smoke was billowing to the heavens, and ashes floated on the gentle breeze. Ham pressed forward along the trail and found a space where he could see to the valley. Two of the cabins lay in a shamble of broken lumber and one was ablaze, the source of the black smoke. Wounded and dead lay on the ground near the cabins. He could see men with buckets trying to put the fire out.

He was too far away to hear what they were saying, but he could hear shouting. Suddenly, two men marched Clyde into the center of the valley and slammed him to his knees near the flag pole.

"Oh shit, Clyde." He leapt from Sundance and ran to a tree with a good vantage point to the bottom. He estimated his distance and raised his rifle, steadying it against the rough pine.

Clyde knew he was cooked. His knees hurt from being slammed down on the rocky ground. His head was pounding from the wallop they'd given him when they captured him. He smiled to himself as he noticed the rope that had until recently tied Betsy to the flagpole. He shook his head as he thought, *Damn dog, best dog I ever had.*

Malik and Nasir approached him and stood silent for a moment as if contemplating his fate.

"You are in a lot of trouble old man," Malik said.

"You're an asshole," Clyde said with a ribald smile and a gravelly sound to his voice.

"Defiant to the end. A great American cowboy, eh?"

"Yes," Nasir agreed. "A real...*John Wayne.*"

"Well, we have business to attend to and you're no longer going to be in our way," Malik said.

"You'll never leave this place...it's the river of no return for you bastards," Clyde threatened.

"It is you, who will not leave this place, and wolves will feast on your bones."

"Looks like the wolves will have plenty to eat," Clyde laughed as he could see them piling the bodies of at least five men he'd killed in his attack.

One of the men standing behind him suddenly punched him in the back of the head. The blow sent Clyde face down into the dirt. The man grabbed the back of his shirt and pulled him back to his knees and then hit him again. Clyde noticed it was the other man who had paid him a visit at the cabin. The one Ham called Leroy.

"Who's on his knees now old man?" he asked with a wicked smile of satisfaction on his face.

"Don't get no ideas. I'm a lady's man," Clyde laughed as blood ran down his face from a cut on his eyebrow.

"You are nothing," Leroy yelled at him.

"That's enough," Malik said with a raised hand. "I'm glad you have decided to sell me your property." He held out a bill of sale to show Clyde.

"No one will believe that."

"Oh, they will. Signed with witnesses, legal in every way. Then you just disappeared," Malik smiled. "Never to be seen again. A strange old hermit lost to the wilds."

"Up your ass with that!" Clyde cursed.

"You're a vile man," Malik said as he motioned to Leroy and raised his hand.

"You're soon to be a dead man," Clyde said.

"No, that's you," Malik said with a nod of his head. He dropped his hand.

156

"No!" Ham yelled into the air. His voice lost to the wind. The man standing behind Clyde pulled a long, sword-style knife from his hip. He raised it high and in one strong downward swing Clyde's head rolled off his shoulders into the dirt. Blood spurting from his neck, his body slumped to the ground.

Ice ran through Ham's veins as a cold anger seized his soul. Ham settled his sights on the man who had swung the blade. He suddenly realized it was Leroy from the diner. He allowed for distance and wind, and squeezed smoothly on the trigger. The sound of the shot echoed over the valley as the recoil impacted Ham's shoulder. The round took Leroy right through the ear, literally exploding the other side of his head with its exit wound. He hit the ground next to Clyde. Dead.

Ham opened fire. Wildly shooting at the valley floor sending them all scattering for cover. When his rifle was empty, he ran to Sundance. He grabbed a box of cartridges from his saddle bags and began thumbing them into his rifle until it was full. He chambered a round and released the hammer. He cocked his head and held his breath. He could hear the sound of four-wheelers climbing up through the trees. He mounted and slapped spurs and leather to Sundance. He lit out like his tail was afire, little Stripey right at his side.

CHAPTER 14

Sundance burst from the trees and thundered across the high plateau. He could sense the trouble, and he was glad to be running for home. Ham cradled the rifle in the crook of his left arm. He glanced over his shoulder, he could see two four-wheelers, each with a driver and a passenger holding a rifle, leaving the tree line and barreling right for him. It was obvious they were going to catch Sundance.

Ham pulled up sharply on the reins sending Sundance onto his haunches skidding to a stop. Ham whirled around and leveled his rifle at the first four-wheeler. He held his breath. His target was bouncing and bobbing with the terrain making for a tough shot. He exhaled and squeezed. Nothing. The shot went high. The man on the four-wheeler began turning abruptly to thwart Ham's shot while the man on the back tried to level his rifle to return fire. Ham heard his shot whiz by over his head.

Ham fired again. The driver's leg exploded with blood. The impact destroyed his thigh bone and the engine block.

He cried out and swerved sharply upending the ATV, sending both the driver and the passenger into the air. The second four-wheeler stopped in its tracks. It was further away than the first one. Ham could see the man trying to get ready for a shot. Ham turned Sundance and put the spurs to him. He was a fast horse and didn't make for an easy shot when he was moving out. Ham hoped they were too far away to hit him. Several shots rang out. One hit the dirt in front of Sundance. Another whirred by Ham's head causing him to involuntarily duck. He kept on running. He heard the engine roar up again from the remaining four-wheeler.

A quick look and he could see one man on foot and the other four-wheeler coming fast. The passenger was snapping off shots at Ham, but none of them were close. Ham whirled Sundance and came around shooting in a cloud of dust.

These two riders had learned from the first. At the sight of Ham turning, they stopped their four-wheeler and jumped for safety, hiding in the tall grass. With no target, Ham continued on after throwing some lead in their direction. The tree line was just up ahead. He was glad for it as Sundance was about done in. He was wet with lather, and Ham could feel the power draining from his muscles with each stride.

The four-wheeler was in pursuit again as they realized Ham was almost to the trees. Ham disappeared into the pines. It felt like going invisible. The cover was a relief, but there was no time to rest as his enemies were coming on hard. He leapt from Sundance and immediately dropped the cinch and grabbed the saddle horn. He ripped it from Sundance's back and tossed it off to the side. He quickly unlatched his bridle and slid it off his head tossing it near the saddle.

Ham waved his arms over his head in Sundance's face and yelled, "Go on! Git! Go on boy! Run!" Sundance was confused at first, but as he turned Ham smacked his rump with his open palm and the horse was gone through the trees with Stripey at his side.

Ham popped off a couple rounds toward the four-wheeler, forcing them to bail off again. Ham turned and ran. The trail back down was mostly rock and too steep for a horse to do in a hurry. He hoped they would follow Sundance for a while until they figured out he was gone. He skidded and slid down the trail scuffing both palms and knees on the jagged rock. He reached the bottom and made for the Hidden Valley. He could hear voices up above him.

He knew if he could get to the mine he could hold them off indefinitely. He was sucking wind as he sprinted past the round pond. He stopped for a quick drink, a splash on his face, and he was off. He climbed the trail through the boulder field, the door to the mine just ahead.

He felt a thump to his hip that sent him falling in a heap. A second shot rang out as he stumbled to his feet and dove through the mine entrance. He slammed the metal door shut as a bullet smashed into it with a wicked ricochet sound. Once it was shut he dug through his pack and put his headlamp on, piercing the darkness. He dropped the heavy timbers into place and effectively barricaded the door.

"They'll have to blow it to get that open," Ham said to himself.

He went to the generator and turned off the gas. It was a simple valve, but it was under the tank and if you didn't know where it was, it would be hard to find. He continued on to the Foreman's Home. He saw the cards on the table and Clyde's glass sitting near his two envelopes. He quickly stuffed the envelopes into his pack and glanced around the room. He grabbed a couple cans of tuna from the shelf and a second canteen full of water and turned to go. His foot kicked something, and he noticed a grenade on the floor.

"Clyde, you shouldn't leave grenades lying around." Ham picked it up with a smile. "This might come in handy."

He froze, listening. Someone was pounding on the metal door. "Good luck, you bastards."

He scurried into the darkness of the mine. His light disappeared down the main shaft as he lowered it manually to the second tunnel. He exited the cage and climbed back up to the first tunnel on the ladder. He went to the back of the tunnel and found the stash. Ammo, some canned food, two pistols, and another rifle. "Thanks, Clyde."

Ham placed them strategically along the shaft. He found the connecting tunnel Clyde had mentioned that would take him between shafts. It was small and not easily discovered. He returned to the front of the tunnel and settled in to wait. He opened a can of tuna and devoured it. He was hungry. He lay his head back. He'd learned to sleep when he could. During a fight, you never knew when your next chance at rest would be.

The pounding ceased on the door to the mine. The silence is what woke him. He sat in complete darkness listening.

Boom! The silence was devastated by a massive explosion that allowed a bit of light to stream in from above. His ears were ringing. They'd blown the door. He had a pistol in each hand. Ready for whatever would come.

He could hear arguing in Arabic from the top of the shaft as they decided what to do. Suddenly, the cage began moving upward. Ham smiled as it went on by his vantage point on its way to the top. They were cranking it up manually. If they came down in that basket, he knew he would have everyone in it dead to rights. Flashlights flashed light down the shaft. The light was swallowed up by the darkness. Ham knew they couldn't see much from the top. The sound of people climbing into the cage and coming back down brought a smile to Ham's face. He stayed well back from the opening to the main shaft.

The men in the cage were shining their beams along the wall looking for him. He knew he'd have to be quick as they'd be ready too, but he had the element of surprise.

The cage dropped down. When it was not quite level with the opening to the shaft Ham stepped forward and opened fire. He could see three men in the cage. Two with pistols and one with a rifle. He was still below them, and they had almost no way to return fire. The roar of the two semi-autos firing was deafening. Ham's first volley hit each man in the cage in the legs. They fell to their knees and began firing randomly. Bullets bounced from wall-to-wall in the shaft. Ham stopped firing as each man in the cage lay atop the other. All three dead.

Ham disappeared into the tunnel like a ghost. They never saw him. Just flashes from the muzzle dealing out death. The cage began going back up. Ham waited till it was almost to the top, and he swung out into the shaft and quickly climbed the ladder down to the second tunnel. He prepared himself for the next assault. They didn't wait. The cage slowly descended. They fired at the opening of the first tunnel to push Ham back inside. He chuckled to himself as he sat safely in the next tunnel down. Suddenly, the entire mine rocked as an explosion echoed through the halls like thunder from hell.

"Son-of-a-bitch!" Ham said as he shook his head. Dust and rock settling down the shaft. He could hear men scurrying around in the upper shaft. Flashes of light bouncing from wall-to-wall through the acrid smoke of guns created an anticipation that death had more to say. The men above him plotted and argued. They were blind, and he still had the upper hand. He wished he knew Arabic. Mac was almost fluent when they killed him. Now it was their turn.

The cage began to descend. Ham figured they would rush the second tunnel just like they had the first. He bolted for the air shaft. It was just past the barracks. He heaved himself up into the tight hole and climbed with all his strength. He bumped his hip against the side wall. It was all he could do not to scream out. Pain like fire exploded as he remembered the shot that had knocked him down at the entrance. He could feel the warm flow of blood, but the tunnel was too tight to do anything about it. He climbed hard as gunfire erupted below him. Just as he pulled himself into the upper tunnel, the mine shook again with another explosion in the second tunnel where he had just been. He sprinted to the mouth of the tunnel. He could see their lights in the main shaft.

A punch in the gut caught him off guard and took his wind. He doubled over and rolled as he hit the ground. He knew a kick would be coming. The man's kick just grazed his face, and he grabbed the foot as it missed. Ham pushed upward with all his might sending his attacker flying head over heels. They both came up in a cloud of dust. The man hollered to his friends something in Arabic. Ham drew his knife and lunged. The man attempted to block his rush with a crossing blow. Ham deflected it. His knife entered the man just above the belt and slid upwards all the way to his sternum, spilling his insides onto the floor.

He continued screaming as his life's blood drained out. Ham ran to the front of the mine. The cage was moving on its way back up. Ham glanced over the edge. He saw four men in the cage. They opened fire at the sight of his head. He jumped back as a barrage of bullets filled the shaft.

Ham pulled the pin on the grenade. "Clyde says fuck you motherfuckers!" Ham tossed it into the shaft. It fell right into the cage and exploded. Silence filled the mine and nothing seemed to be moving. Ham's ears rang as he chanced a look down the shaft. A mess of destroyed body parts and twisted metal was all that was left of the cage and the men in it.

Ham waited. Silence. He took the time to gather himself. His breath returned to normal. The cage was ruined, so he climbed the ladder to the top of the mine. Just as he reached the top, he got a feeling in his gut he didn't like. He undid the strap on his hat and slowly raised it above the edge. Instantly, the room exploded in gunfire. Ham lost his grip and fell back. His foot caught in the ladder and twisted violently. It was all that kept him from falling all the way to the cage.

Ham knew he only had a moment to prepare. He flexed his stomach muscles, ignored a wrenching pain in his side, and grabbed the ladder to free his foot. He pulled his spare pistol from his belt and waited. A light appeared at the top. Slowly, a bearded face peered over the edge. He held steady. The man leaned further over to see down into the shaft.

Bam. A single shot rang out. The man saw the flash of light and then he was falling. He didn't feel anything after that. He was dead before he hit the cage.

Ham climbed up to the ladder and didn't even pause at the top. He was too tired to care. He rolled over and lay on his back. The cool rocky floor felt like a feather bed. No one else was there. He counted back in his head how many men were dead in an attempt to know how many were left. "There can't be more than five or six of them left," he said to himself. "But those top two guys, Malik and Nasir, they got it coming." Ham knew they weren't among the dead. Not yet.

CHAPTER 15

BLOOD

Ham struggled to his feet. His whole body seemed to hurt. His ankle was swollen and already turning black from the fall. His hip was caked with blood. The wound on his head had opened up with fresh blood. All his knuckles were torn and sore. And worst of all, his hat was gone. The war had begun, but it wasn't over.

He peered out of the mine. The metal door lay off to the side mangled from the blast that removed it from its hinges. A gray sunrise was growing to the east. He hobbled back to the Foreman's Home and found a seat at the table laying the first aid kit before him. He wrapped his ankle tightly to immobilize it. Even the wrapping was a brutally painful experience, but pain didn't matter now. There wasn't much he could do for his other wounds. He taped some gauze over the jagged tear the bullet had created on his hip.

He gathered his weapons. Two pistols, his knife, and his rifle was all he had. He checked his ammo count and topped off his magazines. It was all he needed. He drank deep from the water barrel and refilled his canteens. A breakfast of hard bread and a can of cold beef stew from the shelf tasted like a feast. Ham sucked on some salted beef jerky as he headed to the front of the mine. He was ready for a day above ground.

"This is your day, Malik and Nasir. Today is your day for blood," he mumbled to himself.

Ham half expected to be shot as he stepped into the light in front of the mine, but no shot came. Ham couldn't hold back a smile as he saw Sundance and Stripey grazing in the picturesque meadow below as if nothing had happened. Ham wondered what became of Big Jake.

"Probably killed him…like Clyde."

Ham found a bridle in the Foreman's room and staggered down to the meadow. Wrapping the ankle had helped, but walking a long distance on it would be slow and painful.

Sundance trotted over to him and began nuzzling him in search of sugar. Ham put his hand into his pack.

"Your lucky day, buddy. Two left," Ham said as he gave one to Sundance and held out his hand for Stripey to take his. The little zebra nibbled it up as quickly as he could and sprinted away with a kick of his heels.

Ham bridled Sundance and painfully climbed aboard bareback. It seemed his entire body was bruised. His joints ached, and it felt good to ride. The warmth and strength of Sundance's body permeated into Ham with no saddle between them.

He left Hidden Valley behind and followed the woods, keeping off the trails on his way to the main valley. He wanted to get a look at the cabin.

Lloyd sat at the counter eating his eggs in silence. His favorite diner was a busy place this time of year. The river brought in tourists that created a boon for all the local businesses for the season. He liked winter, because his town was like a ghost town. Only locals braved the long cold winter in these parts, and it created a hearty stock of tough folks.

The coffee was hot and black, just the way he liked it. He was thinking of Ham and Clyde while he cut a piece of sausage to dip in his over easy egg. He wondered how they were getting along.

The sheriff and his deputy were eating at a booth behind him near a window looking out to the main street. The bell jingled on the door as two rafters entered. They looked like California twenty-somethings who didn't have a care in the world. Their kind came every summer to float the river, smoke dope, and make love under the stars. They both wore camo embroidered with peace symbols and flowers.

Lloyd had been seeing their kind for decades. They were harmless enough in their ignorance. At the sight of the sheriff, they immediately approached his table. Lloyd noticed and thought that was odd so he listened in while he finished his breakfast seemingly unaware.

"What can I do for you?" the sheriff asked.

"We just floated the river," the young man said.

"Did you have a good time?" the sheriff asked with a friendly smile. Everyone knew he was planning on running for mayor.

"Yeah, it was awesome, but there was a weird thing."

"What kind of weird thing?"

"Well, we floated by this nice-looking beach that had a Keep Out sign."

"Yeah, that's old Clyde's place. He don't like visitors. Some of the beaches are privately owned, but don't let that bother you, there's millions of acres for you out there."

Lloyd was listening intently now.

"Well, around the next turn, we heard these huge explosion sounds, and there was black smoke in the air."

"That's a private summer camp. Probably, just burning some brush."

"It also sounded like gunfire," the girl added.

"Sounds are strange in the canyons. I'm sure it was nothing." The sheriff assured them. "Might have been firecrackers too. You know kids."

"My dad was in the Army. I know what gunfire sounds like," she said confidently.

"Well, we just thought we should tell somebody," the man said.

"Thanks. If you're eating here, all the breakfast is good, or try the tenderloin sandwich, they're the best in the state."

"We don't eat meat," the girl said.

The sheriff shook his head and held back his grin as best he could. She was fulfilling every stereotype the locals had for her. "Well, they have some real nice salads here too, I'm told anyway." The sheriff and the deputy stood to go. "Thanks for coming to the river. You come back sometime and tell your friends." He tipped his hat and followed his deputy out the door.

Lloyd tossed a twenty on the counter and walked out. He drove straight past his house on his way to the airport. The day was clear and bright. Lloyd parked at his hangar and found the kid. "Can you get her ready to go ASAP?" Lloyd asked.

"Didn't know you were coming today. Let me pull her out and top off the tanks for you. Won't take long," the kid answered disappearing to his work.

Lloyd found a seat in the row of chairs out front of the hangar where men usually sat to talk about planes. He searched his smart phone as the kid gassed up the plane. His big fingers looked like sausages pecking at the tiny screen. He found the FBI office in Boise and hit *send*.

"Hello, Federal Bureau of Investigations, how may I help you?" answered a pleasant female voice.

"I want to report a shooting and some explosions," Lloyd said.

"Explosions?"

"Yeah."

"Let me transfer you to a field agent."

He listened to a radio station for two songs as he sat on hold. "Hello, Agent Tucker, how can I help you?"

"I want to report some explosions and gunfire out at the Lost Circus Ranch on the main fork," Lloyd said.

"Did you see anything?"

"I didn't hear it myself, just heard about it from some rafters who heard it."

"Oh, is the person who actually heard it there with you?"

"No."

"Nothing much we can do. Probably just some kids having fun."

"No. There's a jihadi camp out there you know. Training terrorists right by my friend's ranch."

"Whoa, now we have a jihadi camp?"

"That's what I said."

"Yeah, I know the camp you're talking about and just because they're a different religion or nationality doesn't make them terrorists," Agent Tucker sounded condescending.

"Whatever, make a note of it in your file alright?"

"Sure."

"I'm heading out there right now. I will call you if we need help. How fast can you be out there if we need you?"

"Well, we could scramble choppers, but we won't do that for kids goofing around at a summer camp."

"No shit, Sherlock! I'll call if I can. Only if we need you. Clyde has no phone or anything out there."

"Okay. Thanks for calling. What was your name?"

"Lloyd Jenkins, out of Salmon. You better warm up those choppers and get your men ready. I got a feeling about this."

"You got a feeling? Well, you give me a call if your, uh, feeling turns out to be anything."

"I will, you jackass, I'm not kidding."

"You know, I could arrest you for talking to me like that?"

"You can't arrest me for calling you a jackass."

"Threatening a federal officer?"

"Well then, fuck you asshole! I will kick your ass if I ever see you. How's that for a threat? You can fly some birds out to the Lost Circus Ranch and arrest my ass! But you better bring some back up, because I will be the least of your troubles with all those sons-a-bitches out there at your harmless summer camp!"

"You're a difficult old man, aren't you?"

"That's what my wife used to say. Fuel up those choppers. Lloyd out."

Agent Tucker laughed at the phone for a few seconds after Lloyd was gone. Something about old Lloyd was bothering him though. He couldn't tell Lloyd, but their office had been keeping an eye on the *summer camp*. Nothing out of the ordinary had ever been reported, until now. Just for fun he called the hangar.

"Hello, Sampson here."

"It's Tucker. How fast could you have the chopper ready to go out to the main fork of the Salmon in the Church?"

"She's ready now. I just got done giving her a wax and a shine. We're all tired of being on the ground. What are we doing?"

"Nothing, I'll let you know. What team is on duty?"

"Red Team."

"Are they ready?"

"Hell yeah. They're tired of playing ping pong. Let's go!"

"I'll let you know. Thanks Sambo."

Lloyd was sitting in his Cessna waiting for clearance within the hour.

Ham slid from Sundance's back with ease. His ankle throbbed, but it was usable. He didn't have the luxury of worrying about it. He tied the reins gently to a juniper bush, scent of gin in the air. He usually just ground tied him, but Ham wanted to be sure he knew where Sundance was if he came back in a hurry.

He stalked the hillside behind the cabin silently. The trees and brush made for thick cover. He was thankful for it. The ridge above would be dangerous if not for the thick foliage. He glimpsed the cabin through the trees as he edged closer. He paused, listening.

Off in the distance a four-wheeler was approaching. The sound of the engine was getting louder. Ham located it coming down the main trail through the valley. He could see the driver well enough to tell that it wasn't Malik or Nasif. He raised his rifle leaning it against a tree. He kept his bead on the driver. Voices from the cabin caused him to glance quickly to the yard in front of the cabin. Both Malik and Nasif had come out of the cabin to greet the man on the four-wheeler. They stood in the yard not twenty feet from where Betsy had died.

Ham shifted his attention and raised his rifle. The men had stepped behind some trees obscuring his shot. He stood to move to a better vantage point.

"Don't move," a masculine voice with an English accent demanded.

"Damn it," Ham realized he'd been too focused on his targets and allowed this man to get the drop on him.

"Drop the rifle," the voice continued.

Ham turned to face his captor. He was a handsome Arab with a full beard and glasses.

"You're English?" Ham asked as if they were about to become friends. The whole time he was sizing the man up and plotting what he could do to escape.

"I said drop the rifle." The man held an AK in his hands pointed right at Ham's midsection.

Ham leaned the rifle against a tree without taking a step.

"I've been to England before. Great country. Did you grow up there?" Ham continued his questioning.

The man scowled, "Stop asking questions. I went to Oxford and learned my English there. I grew up in Yemen. Now put your hands up. Don't make any moves for that pistol, or I'll shoot you!"

Ham grimaced as he raised his hands, his left shoulder was a painful mess. "I'm sure you will, but that won't be necessary."

"Now we're going to walk down to the cabin," the man directed.

"I'm not. I hurt my ankle really bad."

"You will walk down there, or I'll shoot you"

"No, you won't." Ham had an idea.

"Yes, I will."

"What did you study at Oxford?"

"Shut up about bloody Oxford!"

"I bet it was engineering, or maybe computer programming."

"Electrical engineering," the man said quietly.

"You're supposed to be designing the bombs, I'll bet, not out here in the trees with a rifle?"

The look on the man's face turned to confusion. "I could be working in London…but for the will of Allah."

"I hate to break it to you, but your weapon there, the action is open. It can't fire like that," Ham said with a motion to the rifle in the man's hands.

The man instantly looked down at his weapon. The action was closed correctly. A sinking feeling flashed through his entire body. By the time his eyes raised back to Ham he saw the flash of the shot from the pistol that had been on Ham's hip, but was now firmly in both hands.

The round knocked the man to the ground. It had entered just below his throat on a center line and had destroyed his spine on the way out. Ham approached. He was spitting blood and looked terrified.

"You should've stayed in London," Ham said as he moved on as quickly as he could back toward Sundance. He paused for a look back at the cabin. No one was visible. They'd all taken cover after the shot. It wouldn't be long and they'd be coming.

Ham climbed aboard Sundance and headed away from the cabin, keeping in the trees. There was a thin game trail, and he kept to it. He could hear the sound of a small plane off in the distance.

"Lloyd, oh shit," he said with an eye to the sky.

Lloyd eased down to have a look at Lone Wolf Canyon. He could see one of the cabins had been burned and two others lay in shambles. "Clyde..." he said to himself. No one seemed to be around. After a couple passes he gained altitude and headed for Lost Circus. As he crossed the plateau, he noticed a man who appeared dead lying by an overturned four-wheeler. It was only a few minutes of air time and the big valley came into view. He circled and came back on his landing path. Suddenly, off to the side in the tree line he glimpsed a white horse. He chanced a closer look. He snapped his head just long enough to see it was a disheveled looking Ham. He was waving his hands as if to say *go away*...or was it *help*?

Lloyd was in the glide path now, and he focused his attention on the landing. The earth rose to meet him. Two men stepped from the trees just ahead of him. They didn't wave.

He pulled back hard on the stick as they both raised rifles and began firing. The plane shuddered at the impact. Lloyd heard the rounds ping as they tore metal from the underside of the plane. He kept climbing until he cleared the ridge and was safely away. He could see fuel draining from a hole in the wing to his left.

"Crap. Glad it didn't blow," Lloyd said to himself.

His controls were not responding as they should. It felt as if his tail was wagging, and his altimeter didn't seem to be operating. He immediately began talking into his radio.

"Boise tower, mayday, mayday."

"This is Boise tower, mayday confirm?"

"This is Lloyd Jenkins in Cessna 667498 out of Salmon. My plane has been shot several times, and I'm going down. I'm trying to make it to Johnson Creek field 3U2. I was shot at the

Lost Circus Ranch. I've lost my altimeter and controls are not responding fully, also leaking fuel."

"Repeat. Did you say shot?"

"Yes, shot. Call Agent Tucker at the Boise office of the FBI. Confirm."

"Boise tower, Confirm. Agent Tucker."

"If I'm not at Johnson Creek, look for me somewhere between there and Lost Circus. I'm gonna try to make it, 498 out."

"Boise tower out."

A minute later Agent Tucker's phone rang. Within a half an hour, Sampson had his headset on and was firing up his black chopper. Agent Tucker and the four-man Red Team sat in back, locked and loaded.

"Sambo, what's our estimated flight time?" Agent Tucker asked through the radio.

"Estimated 56 minutes."

"Thanks. Red Team ready."

CHAPTER 16

CHOPPER

Ham watched as Lloyd flew away. "Well, we're on the clock now." Sundance flicked an ear as if listening. "Lloyd will call in the Cavalry." They continued on until they reached the deep woods along the hog kill zone. Ham dismounted and found a rock to lay prone upon, scanning the valley with his binoculars.

He heard the four-wheeler before he saw it. Two men rode the four-wheeler while two others walked. They were arrayed across the field of grass as if they were bird hunting. Each carried a rifle. Ham snapped off a couple rounds in their direction. They were out of range, but he wanted to slow them down as he came up with a plan.

The men disappeared into the tall grass taking cover.

Ham thought he could pick them off one at a time if they were determined to stay in the open field. Or he could make a break for it on Sundance. They couldn't follow the trail on the four-wheeler. On foot, Sundance could leave them behind easily. He could probably hole up at #2 and wait for help.

He pulled out his binocs and glassed the men in the field. They were cautiously coming out from their hiding positions. Ham could see both Malik and Nasir were among them. They were the two on the four-wheeler. The other two men, he didn't know their names, foot soldiers.

He raised his rifle and sighted Nasir as he climbed aboard the four-wheeler once again. He fired. The shot hit the four-wheeler sending Nasir to the ground once again. Ham smiled at the good luck of his shot. The two men on the edges were crawling through the grass. He noticed one of them, but then lost him again. The grass was providing good cover for them. Ham knew he had to move or they would get in close enough to triangulate him.

Ham fired a couple shots where he guessed the crawlers might be and then hurried back to Sundance. The two men on the ground suddenly stood and began firing in his direction. They were closer than Ham had thought. Bullets whizzed by his head and hit the surrounding trees. Duck and cover.

Ham heard the four-wheeler racing forward amidst the firing. He knew they were coming for him. He swung his bad leg up and over Sundance and lit out through the trees. He fired a couple shots back toward the field as he disappeared from view.

As much as he wanted to kill Malik and Nasir, he was tired, outnumbered, and on the run. The wise thing to do would be skin out. He thought of Clyde. He knew Clyde would say something like, "See ya later. I'm fuckin' stayin' to kill them sonsabitches!".

He continued on for a half hour. He realized that he had an opportunity to double back on his pursuers. They might not see him before he was past them, and he could head for the main cabin. Since they were on foot, he could make a stand from the cabin. With any luck, maybe Malik and Nasir would make a mistake and he could take them out and not get whacked himself. He whirled Sundance and turned back down the treed side of the slope. He hit the open field at a full run.

He smiled. They hadn't expected that. He was half way to the pond before they snapped a shot at him, and he was well out of range.

Ham pulled Sundance up at the pond and let him drink while he scanned the terrain with the binocs. He could see them standing together in the trees talking. It started in the distance at first, but now there was no denying the sound of an approaching chopper. The welcome sound of a warbird…he'd heard a thousand times before.

"Air CAV," he whispered. The black attack helicopter circled the field several times locating the men below. It zeroed in on the men with AK's having a chat in the field. The chopper took an offensive posture, pointing its on board weapons in their direction.

Ham saw the men put down their weapons and raise their hands up.

He exhaled loudly, "It's over." He gave Sundance a kick and he cantered toward the chopper at a leisurely lope. The chopper landed and shut down its blades. They slowly spun to stop and the sounds of the field returned. A creek babbled not far off and birds called the trees. Four men in full battle gear dismounted the open side door of the chopper, fanning out to surround the men surrendering.

Ham dismounted and raised his own hands. No need to get shot by mistake. They corralled them all together. Ham stood next to Malik and glared at him.

One of them from the chopper spoke, "What's going on fellas? Havin' an argument, are we?"

Malik glanced at Nasir, and they shared a knowing nod as if they were up to something. Ham took a step toward Malik.

"Stop right there," the man from the chopper commanded. "I'm Agent Tucker, and you are all under arrest until we figure this out."

Malik stepped in close to Ham. "Your friend died like a pig, begging for his life like a child."

"Bullshit," Ham said.

"I said, knock it off," agent Tucker said. "Step back!"

Malik stared only at Ham, as if they were alone. "Like a little girl."

Ham swung a quick jab that caught Malik on the cheek. Malik leaned into it and grabbed Ham by the shoulder pulling him toward him. Ham saw the blade flash. Too late. It slid between two ribs until the hilt was tight against Ham's body. Ham endured a blinding pain as if his side was on fire. He felt like he might vomit as his wind was knocked out of him from his lung collapsing.

Nasir burst into a sprint toward the chopper. He made it past the guard closest to him and was closing on the chopper. One of the other Red Team members opened fire. Several shots hit Nasir and as he staggered forward he screamed, "Allahu Ak…" He was wearing an explosive vest and as he fell he hit the trigger mechanism. He exploded into a million pieces.

Malik stood over Ham as he fell to the ground still glaring into his eyes, "Say hello to your friend in hell."

"You first." Malik hadn't noticed the pistol in Ham's right hand. Ham fired a single shot. The round took Malik in the forehead, the back of his skull exploding in a spray of red mist. He shuddered and collapsed face first to the ground next to Ham. Ham lay back and let the pistol fall from his grip.

The last two men raised their hands high.

"Secure them," Agent Tucker commanded. They were handcuffed and loaded into the chopper.

Agent Tucker knelt by Ham. "You alright?"

"I've been better," Ham replied. He coughed up blood.

"Well, you're safe now. We got you."

Red Team placed Ham on a backboard and upon loading into the chopper began working on his wound to minimize the bleeding.

Ham grabbed Agent Tucker's arm. "Take the bridle off Sundance, my horse. He'll be fine if you do that."

The pilot looked toward the white horse dragging his reins around as he grazed.

He noticed Sundance's companion. "Is that a zebra?"

"Stripey, yeah, it's a long story," Ham said with a grimace.

The pilot ran over to Sundance and quickly removed the bridle, tossing it to the ground. He ran back to the chopper. He noticed that the side of it was covered in bits of Nasir.

"Damn, that guy got my chopper dirty with his guts!"

He quickly climbed into his seat and Sambo began his process for takeoff. The blades rotated slowly at first, accelerating until they were a spinning blur. Ham could see that the agent who was closest to Nasir was bleeding. Shrapnel had cut his face and shoulder. They had his shirt off and were working on him.

Ham's chest felt like a ton of bricks had been placed on it. He felt the chopper lift off as he struggled to hold off the need to puke. He was queasy, then suddenly everything went dark.

Ham heard someone yell, "Gimme an IV! He's lost a lot of blood."

Ham's eyes opened. He blinked them repeatedly to bring them into focus. Everything was white, and clean. He heard monitors beeping and could feel needles in both arms. He had no shirt on and half his side was covered in bandages. He saw a girl with dark hair asleep in the chair in the corner.

"Julie?"

She snapped awake. She rushed to the open door and yelled into the hall, "He's awake!"

She returned to his side, a smile across her face.

"What are you doing here?" Ham asked with a raspy voice.

Julie looked down and a little dejected. "I can go if you want me to."

"No, don't go."

"They found my card in your things. They didn't have anyone else to call, so they called me. Here I am. I've been dreaming what I should say right now, and now I'm not saying anything. I'm just standing here...and I'm so glad you're awake. I thought you might die and I didn't know what to..."

She was talking fast as she was obviously nervous.

Ham raised his hand to stop her. She did. He just stared at her in disbelief.

"Well, say something?" she said.

"Come here." He motioned for her to come towards him.

She stepped closer. He raised one hand with wires attached to it and pulled her close. He kissed her deeply on the lips.

After they were done, she stepped back, and gasped for a breath. She flashed a coy smile.

"You should be careful about your IV," she said, her face flush with color.

"I'm glad you're here. I've been thinking about you ever since I left. Every day."

"Really? I've thought of you too," she said with a sheepish smile. "Lloyd said you were a fighter and not to worry...you were gonna be fine, but they said you were stabbed only a centimeter from your heart and your lung…"

"Lloyd? Is he alright?"

"I'm fine, my plane is not so lucky," Lloyd said as he entered the room. He stepped near to Ham's bed and looked down at him. They locked eyes.

"I'm sorry about Clyde," Ham said.

Lloyd looked away and took the seat in the corner. "I'd love to hear that story. The story of Clyde's demise. A good one for a fireside tale, I'll bet?"

"Definitely," Ham said with a grin. "He went out like he lived."

"And with a bang," Lloyd agreed.

"A big fuckin' bang," Ham added with a smile. "Remember the grenades you got him for blowing beaver dams?"

A nurse stepped in, "How are you feeling?"

"Thirsty," Ham answered. "I'll take a beer."

"Ha, ha, very funny. I can bring you a water or ice chips. Sorry, we're short staffed. I'll be right back though," she answered.

"No problem, I've got my friends here."

"Great," she said as she disappeared down the hall.

Lloyd stood and handed Clyde's envelope to Ham. "I already read mine, so go ahead. Open it up."

"Alright," Ham said tearing the seal. He read it quickly. It was short and to the point, just like Clyde.

Dear Ham, if you're reading this I am gone. I hope I went out with my boots on. Either way, I am giving you the Lost Circus Ranch as Ox gave it to me. I have no heirs, and I would give it to my good friend Lloyd, but he's as old as dirt. You're young, and you can make something good of the ranch again. If possible, I would like to be buried in

the field by Ox. It's as good a place as any for old bones.
Take care of Betsy for me. She's the best dog I ever had.
My only request is that you take care of Lloyd in his old
age with the "crop". Don't worry, he won't live too much
longer. Anyway, I am dead. The ranch was a great place to
live. Now it is yours.

Your friend, Clyde.

"He gave me the will that signs it over legal and all. It's yours," Lloyd said. "What you gonna do with it?"

"I don't know," he glanced at Julie. "Show it to Julie first, I guess. See what she thinks...the ranch has lots of potential for all kinds of things." She smiled at Ham and grabbed his hand.

"Sounds like a plan. Speaking of taking care of old Lloyd, I might need some of that 'crop' to fix my plane. I left her out at Johnson Creek all shot up," Lloyd said with a smile.

"I'm not even out of the hospital, and it starts already," Ham said with a laugh. "No problem. How about a whole new plane? Anything for my friend Lloyd."

ABOUT THE AUTHOR

 S.C. "Steve" Sherman grew up an Iowa farm kid. He still lives and works in Hawkeye country with his wife, Amy, and their four children, Mollie, Cole, Brock, and Sariah. Steve is the Senior Editor at *DailySurge.com* and is a sought-after speaker and guest on radio and TV. Steve loves outdoor activities and larger than life stories. He has written across several genres pushing the envelope of political correctness with each one. His novels include: *Leaving Southfields*, a historical fiction; *Hell and Back*, a spiritual thriller; *Moxie*, a young adult fantasy; and *Mercy Shot*, a political thriller.

For more information about
S.C. Sherman
and to order books or schedule a speaking event go to:
www.scsherman.com
steve@scsherman.com
www.facebook.com/scsherman